Sale

W9-CGU-074

JEANMARIE
and the Missing Ring

JEANMARIE
and the Missing Ring

APPLE VALLEY
MYSTERIES

Lucille Travis

Baker Books

A Division of Baker Book House Co
Grand Rapids, Michigan 49516

© 2001 by Lucille Travis

Published by Baker Books
a division of Baker Book House Company
P.O. Box 6287, Grand Rapids, MI 49516-6287

Printed in the United States of America

All rights reserved. No part of this publication may be reproduced, stored in a retrieval system, or transmitted in any form or by any means—for example, electronic, photocopy, recording—without the prior written permission of the publisher. The only exception is brief quotations in printed reviews.

Library of Congress Cataloging-in-Publication Data

Travis, Lucille, 1931–
    Jeanmarie and the missing ring / Lucille Travis.
       p.   cm.—(Apple Valley mysteries)
    Summary: In 1945, the girls at Apple Valley Orphanage believe the quiet new Jewish girl is stealing stamps and other small objects, and that their housemother is being threatened by a strange man.
    ISBN 0-8010-4487-1 (paper)
    [1. Orphans—Fiction. 2. Stealing—Fiction. 3. Jews—United States—Fiction. 4. Christian life—Fiction. 5. Mystery and detective stories.] I. Title. II. Series.
PZ7.T68915 Jd 2001
[Fic]—dc21
                                    2001043190

For current information about all releases from Baker Book House, visit our web site:
              http://www.bakerbooks.com

For Montana,
the newest treasure
in our family

Contents

Sophie

Sophie stood at the window and let her hands slide down the cold iron bars that kept out the city below. The Children's Shelter with its barred windows and metal doors seemed more like a jail than a place where children were sent to wait until their cases were heard in the county court next door. Being locked inside made Sophie feel that she was somehow guilty of something besides being an orphan. Thoughts of her mama and papa brought tears that threatened to spill over.

If only they hadn't left her alone in this world. "I don't even have a picture of you, Mama," she whispered. Papa had always said she looked just like her mother—wine-red hair that curled every which way and eyes, he said, "so blue-green they made the spring jealous." Sophie's lips lifted briefly in a half-smile before her thoughts turned once more to the present.

What would the orphanage be like that the judge sent her to after deciding her case? For two weeks she had lived in this shelter waiting for her name to be called. At night she slept in a large dormitory that had long rows of iron cots. Each morning she and the other girls swept and mopped every floor with large-handled mops and brooms almost too heavy to push. Since there was no teacher for the one-room classroom they spent the rest of the day in a great empty room lined with benches. The youngest children played on the floor with the few toys provided. Older girls stood around or sat in little groups talking. From a chair in front of the door a matron watched until meal times. Sophie desperately wanted to leave.

"Hey, Red." Sophie turned toward the voice. The big girl standing near one of the barred windows had taken to calling her Red thanks to her hair. "Hurry up if you want to see what the judge looks like."

Sophie looked to where the girl pointed at the street below. A figure in a dark suit and hat strode up the courthouse steps and disappeared inside. It was too far to see the man's face.

"That's the judge. And I'm telling you, Red, the man's got no heart. Send you upriver to one of them homes for delinquents quick as a wink," the girl said. "Course, you're one of the lucky ones." She gave Sophie a hard look. "Unless you been in trouble and got some kind of record, you'll be sent off to an orphanage. That's a lot better than where I'm probably going." The girl looked back at the street.

Sophie wondered if the judge ever made mistakes. She hadn't done anything really bad. Nervously she fingered the small silver Star of David on the chain around her neck. Bad things could happen to Jewish children. She had seen the war newsreels that showed endless lines of Jewish families being marched off to work camps, yellow Stars of David sewn to their coats. Maybe she would not wear her necklace into the courthouse. Maybe she would not wear it ever again.

That night in the darkness a small figure dressed in a thin nightgown walked past the rows of cots. As the figure neared the door someone whispered loudly, "Red; hey, Red! What do you think you're doing?"

Sophie woke with a start and stared at her bare feet on the cold floor near the metal door. How had she gotten here? She'd been dreaming about the war, and the next thing she knew she'd awakened standing here.

Back in her cot Sophie pulled the covers close to her chin to stop her shivering. Now she remembered her dream and the long lines of Jewish children. She had been one of them! "Oh, Mama, Papa, I need you. Why did you have to die?" Tears flowed down her face. Why couldn't she have died in that car accident too?

She reached under her pillow, searching until she found the small metal star. Clutching it tightly to her chest she moaned softly.

ONE

An Inside Thief

Wind blew hard, cold rain against gray tree trunks and rattled through the drafty windows of the orphanage as if to hide the fact that spring had finally arrived. Inside Wheelock Cottage for girls Jeanmarie pulled the sleeves of last year's sweater down as far as she could. The old brown sweater went well with her brown braided hair and eyes but would soon have to go. The chill inside and the dark overcast sky above the Apple Valley Orphanage grounds only deepened the gloom Jeanmarie felt. The faces of the four girls seated on the dorm floor near her wore similar glum looks.

"The only stamp I had is missing," Jeanmarie said in a low voice. For the third week in a row things had gone missing from each of the girls in the dorm. At first they'd thought it was some kind of joke, but it wasn't funny anymore. The orphanage only allowed the girls a few personal things. "No outsider could get into our stuff," Jeanmarie said, looking at the others who all shared the dorm. "It has to be someone on the inside, and it's not one of us. We've each lost things we needed, and it keeps happening," she said. "Whoever is doing this has to be right under our noses, and we don't have a clue." She did not say the thought that crossed her mind. Not yet.

Sighing deeply, Winnie pushed a lock of thin blonde hair behind her ear. Her round, pale face looked pained. "If it's not any of us, that doesn't leave too many choices unless somebody really is breaking into Wheelock. I know that sounds too crazy," she added. Seated on the floor beside her Tess and Maria laughed together in the peculiar way of identical twins. Except for the small dark mole near Maria's mouth their faces were alike, their black curls and dark eyes exact copies of each other's.

Winnie frowned. "Don't forget the time that patient from Letchworth mental institution got into our basement and stole all the boots. Still, I don't think they'd dare keep coming back. Anyway, nothing is funny about this. We have a war going on, and anyone stealing things is just, well, just not patriotic," she said, her voice somber.

Tess reached out and patted Winnie's arm. "It's serious," she said. "We've all lost things we counted on. Nothing like this has happened before as long as we've been here." Tess looked thoughtful. "What I don't understand is why the thief doesn't take things like jewelry or anything. So far it's all been practical items like stamps, ribbons, pins, spools of thread, pencils, paper clips, bobby pins, an eraser, even the foil wrappers I was saving for the scrap drive."

"Right," Pearl said, her freckled face thoughtful in spite of the unruly cloud of short brown hair that gave her the appearance of a carefree street urchin. "It's strange."

Jeanmarie rested her elbows on her knees, her chin in her hands. "I was saving that stamp just in case." Her throat tightened. Unlike the other orphans, Jeanmarie was a ward of the state even though both her parents were living. Somewhere she had a mom, and she never knew when her mom would write to let her know where she was. Few as the letters were, she tried to answer them quickly before her mother moved on again. Now she wouldn't have another stamp until next month.

Once a month the orphanage allowed purchases from its small store—items like stamps and writing paper and the usual candy. Miss Bigler, assistant to Dr. Werner, the superintendent of the orphanage, kept a record of the girls' earnings. The orphanage paid two and a half cents an hour for their work after school. Whatever they bought was deducted from their wages.

Maria shook her head sadly as Tess sighed. "Sorry; we used our only stamp a week ago," she said.

"And since I never need any I don't have one to lend you," Pearl added.

Jeanmarie heard the note of pain in Pearl's voice. Months ago Pearl had lost her only living relative, an aunt. Jeanmarie swallowed hard. She made her voice light. "I probably won't get a letter for months, and by that time I'll be ready. Anyway, right now the first thing we need to do is find out who our thief is and how to catch him," she said. "Her," she corrected herself.

"Well, it makes me mad," Tess said, her dark eyes flashing, "to think that someone is stealing instead of just asking to borrow. And now none of us has anything left to lend."

Jeanmarie thought hard. Her mind was already forming a plan. "We can cross off the little girls from our list," she said. "They've never done anything like it before. And none of the new attic girls would bother." The three older orphans were high-school seniors who had their own little world in the attic where they slept and studied. "Besides, all of them work every day off grounds," she added. "That leaves Leah and the new girl." She paused to let her words sink in. "We started noticing things were disappearing three weeks ago. The only new person around here is Sophie. The first thefts started a week after she came." Jeanmarie pressed her lips together and waited.

Pearl looked startled. "Sophie? I could imagine Leah. Old habits are hard to change, and she used to be a real troublemaker before her buddy Emma moved away. But Sophie? Her father was a chaplain and a war hero before he died."

Winnie nodded in agreement. "Right, and her mother was a war nurse who died in the same battle as her father. Poor things. Sophie said they died in France."

"Not France, Win; they were in Italy," Maria corrected. "Her mother drove an ambulance, the very one that her father and mother died in. So sad isn't it, losing her folks both at the same time and far away on a battlefield."

"But it was France," Pearl said. "I heard her tell Winnie it was France. She said a bomb hit the trench where her father was just as he was trying to help a fellow soldier. Her mother died in the same battle."

"But she did say Italy when she told Maria and me about the ambulance," Tess said in a puzzled tone. "Maybe her father was only badly wounded when they put him in the ambulance, and then her mother, who was driving, was killed along with him when the bomb hit."

"Right," Pearl agreed. "From Italy they must have driven across the border into France trying to get to the camp hospital; so that explains it. Anyway, she asked me for a stamp just the other day. Why would she do that if she already had one of ours? It shows she's not the one."

"Unless she asked for the stamp so no one would suspect her," Jeanmarie said quietly. A knock at the open door interrupted her.

Mrs. Ripple, the housemother, stood framed in the doorway, her silver blonde hair wound in braids about her head like a halo. Her generally white, starched apron looked slightly crumpled. "Girls, have any of you seen my small scissors or a black leather change purse? I seem to have mislaid them, though I thought I left them on the parlor table." A small frown wrinkled her forehead. No one answered. "No? Well then, please keep your eyes open for them. I'm sure they'll turn up somewhere." With that she left.

Her words hung in the air. "So now Mrs. Ripple is missing things," Pearl said quietly. "I don't think those scissors or that change purse are anywhere we'll find soon."

A coughing spell gripped Winnie, the hard, in-the-chest kind of cough. Though Winnie looked stockier than any of them, she was the frailest among them and never far from a cold or fever. In a thin voice she added, "We can't go to Mrs. Ripple and accuse anyone of stealing without evidence, real proof. She wouldn't listen."

Jeanmarie patted Winnie's arm. It was true. Mrs. Ripple was strict, but she was fair. "You're right, Win. And besides, if we go to her about our stuff, suppose she does call in Dr. Werner? We don't want him involved or we'll all be on restrictions until someone confesses." Restrictions meant no passes for Sunday walks off grounds, no Saturday night events, no listening to the radio, or anything else that might be considered privileges. Her mind was made up. "We can handle this ourselves," she said.

Bending her head above the paper in her hand, Jeanmarie began writing as the others gathered closer. "It means setting up a watch. Since we have to start somewhere, we might as well begin with Sophie." At the look on Pearl's face, she quickly added, "Sophie moved in last, and we'll just be working our way down the list." After Sophie's name came Leah's followed by a large question mark. They were the only two on the list so far. She held the paper out to the others. In her heart she felt certain the trouble had begun with the new girl, Sophie.

Unaware of the plan forming for her, Sophie sat on the cot assigned to her in the corner of the small dorm she shared with a girl named Leah and the younger girls. At the moment the dorm was empty. In spite of her resolve to be strong Sophie felt a weariness wash over her as tears threatened to spill. She dabbed at her eyes with the edge of the spread. "I miss you, Mama." She tried to picture the room that had been her home; she remembered the peg behind the door where her father's prayer shawl and her mother's apron hung. "Papa, you worked so hard in old Herman's tailor shop, but if only you hadn't taken Mama to work with you that day I wouldn't be here," she wailed. "Why didn't you look before you crossed the street; why, Papa?" She sobbed quietly, covering her face with her hands.

Long after lights-out Jeanmarie lay on her cot wide awake. From the sounds of soft breathing she knew the others were asleep. At the foot of her bed a gust of wind lifted the heavy blackout curtain. Air-raid drills and blackout curtains, thanks to the war, had become part of life in the orphanage. What she needed was a drink of water. Her bare feet made little noise on the wooden floor in the long hall that led to the washroom. Behind her the night-light from the small bathroom reserved for the younger girls cast a feeble light. She made her way to the landing at the top of the staircase where the hall turned right and led to the larger washroom. She was almost there when a sound made her stop. At the end of the hallway ahead of her light was glowing from Mrs. Ripple's sewing room. The sounds seemed to be coming from there.

Tiptoeing closer toward the half-open door she flattened herself against the wall. Someone was crying. Holding her breath Jeanmarie peered through the crack between the door and the wall.

Mrs. Ripple, seated at her table with her head bowed, her hands clasped, wept as though her heart would break. Suddenly in a choked voice she cried out, "It is so hard to bear."

Startled, Jeanmarie backed away, nearly stumbling in her haste. Had Mrs. Ripple gotten a telegram from the War Office? Had somebody died in the war, or worse still, were they missing in action? She'd never seen Mrs. Ripple like this. From the start when she'd come to replace their old housemother, Mrs. Ripple had sailed in like a strong, sturdy ship, someone you could count on.

Back in her cot once again, Jeanmarie pulled the blanket up to her chin. In her years at the orphanage she had known more than one housemother and heard of others. Mrs. Ripple was one of the good ones, strict but fair. What could have happened? Nothing she knew of at the orphanage, only the thefts. Jeanmarie plumped her pillow and started to burrow into it but sat up instead. She'd remembered Mrs. Ripple's missing change purse and small scissors. What if something else was missing? Something Mrs. Ripple hadn't told them about. A thing so important that she couldn't bear losing it? Maybe the thefts weren't just about little things anymore. Sophie's face flashed before her mind.

TWO

Burnt Soup

Sunlight shining through the open window dappled the floor at the foot of Jeanmarie's bed and warmed her bare feet as she dressed. Quickly she slid her work dress over her head, tied the belt, and smoothed its faded cotton skirt once bright with small yellow and green flowers. Saturday breakfast came a little later than on weekdays, enough time to tell Pearl and the others about last night.

Seated on the floor in the farthest corner of the dorm with the door partly closed, Jeanmarie told the others what she had seen. It sounded so strange that for a moment Jeanmarie thought she might have dreamed hearing Mrs. Ripple cry, but only for a moment.

"Dr. Werner would deliver anything from the War Office himself," Maria said. "All the mail from servicemen has an official War Department stamp on the envelope; I'd have noticed." Maria, who worked at the

Werners' house, generally brought home any mail for Mrs. Ripple.

Winnie's eyes grew wide. "You don't think she has a terrible illness, do you? I mean a serious kind of thing that she doesn't want us to know about."

"She doesn't act or look sick to me," Jeanmarie said. "What if she's missing something really valuable, not just the change purse and scissors? Something she can't bear to lose, and she feels terrible to think one of us may have taken it."

"If she thought one of us stole from her," Pearl said, "then why hasn't she marched us all together into the parlor for a meeting and one big showdown? Wouldn't she try to find out who it is? I mean before she just gave up?"

Jeanmarie sighed. "I guess you're right. She doesn't know we have a thief. But if it isn't something Mrs. Ripple's lost that's upset her, then that leaves us with two mysteries on our hands—the thief we haven't caught yet and whatever caused Mrs. Ripple to cry last night."

Pearl looked thoughtful. "So far we don't have a clue."

Jeanmarie frowned. "That's all the more reason for sticking with our plan. We need to clear up the first problem and fast." She looked around at the group. "As soon as morning chores are finished we can start watching Sophie's every move for the rest of the day. This morning it will have to be Pearl and me, since it's Saturday and we'll be working off grounds this afternoon while the rest of you are here." A Jewish family who'd moved into their summer cottage early had requested Saturday household help from the orphanage. Miss Bigler had assigned Jeanmarie and Pearl.

Winnie spoke up. "Don't worry; I'll take the afternoon watch. Maybe I'll get Sophie to talk to me and find out something useful." Winnie's soft voice sounded hopeful.

"I can take over after supper," Tess offered. "Together Maria and I could hang around from a distance. We don't want Sophie to start wondering why all the sudden interest when she's made it plain she likes being by herself."

"Right," Maria said. "I was thinking the same thing." She grinned at her twin, who grinned back. Jeanmarie smiled. The twins often did think alike.

"Good," she said. "That's settled then." She stood up. "We'd better go down and see what's happening." After last night she had no idea what to expect from Mrs. Ripple this morning.

Standing near the breakfast table Mrs. Ripple greeted the girls with a smile. Jeanmarie searched her face but saw no sign that anything had happened the night before. Pearl looked at her questioningly, but Winnie whispered, "Poor thing. It's just like her to put on a brave front."

For a moment Jeanmarie studied Winnie's face with its gentle blue eyes, its look of concern. Did Winnie see something she didn't? If anyone knew about sickness, it was Winnie. They'd almost lost her last winter. "Keep an eye on her, Win," she whispered back.

The oatmeal had cooled by the time Jeanmarie tasted it. She ate her slice of toast and washed it down with milk. Across the room Sophie, the new girl, sat silent, her face unsmiling, her red hair brushed out like a thick bush around her head. For an instant her eyes met Jeanmarie's, then quickly turned away. But Jeanmarie had seen just a flash of something. Guilt? Fear? Whatever it was Sophie didn't look her way again.

"She doesn't seem to want to fit in," Pearl said in a low voice. "The only thing we know about her is what she said about her folks. Guess I'd brag too if I knew mine were war heroes. But I don't think she's made any friends."

Jeanmarie pushed her half-filled oatmeal bowl away. "Maybe it's because she doesn't dare as long as she's stealing from us." She shouldn't accuse anyone without proof, she thought, but who else could it be? Leah had sworn friendship months ago, and nothing had happened to change that.

"Okay," Maria whispered, "we'll just watch and see."

The morning went quickly, and neither Jeanmarie nor Pearl had seen anything suspicious in Sophie's movements. Reluctantly they'd left for work after lunch. The day felt warm. The road to the Jewish family's cottage wound through a small wooded area a mile from the orphanage grounds. Every tree trunk glistened from yesterday's hard rain. Jeanmarie bent to pluck a spray of wild columbine, its flowers like small red hats stuffed with yellow hair. Pearl picked small white flowers on slender stems above a bed of dark green leaves. "Looks like paperwhites," she said, tucking them into her hair behind her ear. "I could go on walking here in the woods all day, but there's our cottage and all those dishes waiting." Pearl arranged the blossoms as they went up the narrow path to the white house with its red door and bright red and yellow curtains in the front windows.

The gray-haired woman who opened the door smiled broadly, revealing her gold tooth, as she greeted them. Pearl held out the flowers. Mrs. Shapiro's face beamed with delight as she took them. "Beautiful, no? Thank you, children. So, like before, you come right on time. And last week such good workers you are, my son said, 'We should have help like this back in the city, no?'" She turned a grandmotherly look of concern on the girls. "But so far you have walked, you must eat something first before you start, yes?"

Jeanmarie smiled as they followed Mrs. Shapiro back into the small kitchen. The family had already eaten their Sabbath meal, and dishes lay strewn on the table, pots on the stove with leftovers still in them. She and Pearl were to clear away everything, tidy the kitchen, mop the floor, and vacuum the front room and the hallway. Pearl took a cookie from the tray left for them, and Jeanmarie chose a small prune-filled bun. "Such a little bit; come take more," Mrs. Shapiro urged. She pointed to the cookie tray. "Here; I leave this all for you, so you help yourself, please." With a gentle pat on Jeanmarie's shoulder she left the kitchen. Jeanmarie had no idea where the rest of the family were while she and Pearl worked. They had only met Mrs. Shapiro's son and daughter-in-law once. Last week Mrs. Shapiro had sat on the front porch with her company and left the two girls alone until they'd finished their work.

While Pearl dried and Jeanmarie washed the last of the dirty pots, Pearl said, "Funny, isn't it, how their Saturdays are like our Sundays? Course we still do dishes and clean up the kitchen Sundays or not."

"If they weren't Jewish we might not have this job," Jeanmarie said. "Mrs. Ripple says some Jewish people don't believe in doing any work at all on the Sabbath, not even cooking or turning off a light switch, but the Shapiros aren't that strict. Anyway, they were glad to hire us to do most of it."

While Pearl cleaned the front room, Jeanmarie mopped the kitchen. She had just finished and started on the hallway leading to the porch when she found herself face-to-face with a small boy of about seven. His black eyes stared at her blankly, his thin face too white for a healthy boy. Before Jeanmarie could say a word he ran out onto the porch and away into the woods. For a minute she watched him go until he disappeared behind the trees. She didn't mean to eavesdrop on Mrs. Shapiro and her company who were sitting just out of sight where the porch turned to the shady side of the cottage.

"I don't know what I'm going to do with that boy, and him my only grandson." The voice speaking in a sharp tone belonged to Mrs. Shapiro's friend. "Night after night he has the same nightmares. Such a thing, you wouldn't believe. He wakes up screaming and won't go back to bed in his room.

Not that I mind him sleeping with me. He doesn't remember his dreams, he says."

Mrs. Shapiro's voice drifted back to Jeanmarie. "But, Hannah dear, such a thing must mean something is troubling the child."

"I do not know what, Ada. He won't talk about it. Back in the city he doesn't go outside alone, doesn't want to play with the children in the building. He follows me everywhere, like a little burr stuck to the coat. He's bright, that one, listens to everything, always watching with those big eyes and listening. The worst thing is the sleepwalking."

"Oh no!" Mrs. Shapiro exclaimed. "You don't mean to say the child walks in his sleep?"

In a solemn tone, her visitor replied, "Once right out of the kitchen and down the stairs before I found him. It's a sickness; the good rabbi says maybe he'll grow out of it. So meanwhile we just watch."

"And hope nothing happens to the poor boy, like he breaks a leg or some terrible thing." Mrs. Shapiro sounded distressed. "My poor Hannah, such a burden for you."

Her company's voice rose to a shrill note in agreement. "Oy vey, sometimes I think it is those lost in this terrible war that he sees in his dreams. So many gone in Germany—Aunt Golda, Uncle Sol, so many many we will never see again." Her voice ended on a sob.

"No; no, Hannah. These are terrible times for our Jewish race, but there is always hope that we will find our relatives somewhere outside of Germany safe and waiting for the war to end."

Jeanmarie swished her mop across the floor and made her way back toward the kitchen. She'd heard about the cruel treatment of the Jewish people in Germany under Hitler and his Nazis. She was glad the Allies were fighting Hitler and his troops. Emptying her pail she thought of the boy who had nightmares and walked in his sleep. It troubled her. What would make a little boy so upset?

On the way home with fifty cents in her pocket and munching on cookies from Mrs. Shapiro, Jeanmarie told Pearl about the boy. "That's it," she said, "and whatever is making him like that is a mystery to his folks."

"Sad," Pearl said. Her voice changed abruptly, dropping almost to a whisper. "Don't stare," she said, "but isn't that the new farmer's son walking ahead of us just behind that first row of maples?"

Jeanmarie looked in time to see a tall thin boy, loping along with a rifle on his shoulder, glance back in their direction. He waved and a moment later disappeared into the woods. "It's him," she said. "He must be out hunting." The farmer and his family had moved into a cottage on the orphanage grounds a month ago. Twice the boy, Ralph, had come to a Saturday night square dance at the orphanage gym. Once he and Jeanmarie had ended up as partners. She thought of his red face and shy look. When he tripped over his own large feet, he'd laughed with a laugh that began at his toes and built up all through his lanky frame. With a start Jeanmarie realized she hadn't heard a word Pearl was saying.

As the two girls neared Wheelock Cottage Maria hurried toward them, waving a letter in her hand. "For Mrs. Ripple!" she called.

Mail at the orphanage always caused excitement since few of the orphans ever had any. Jeanmarie glanced at the envelope in Maria's hand. There was no return address. "I can take the letter," she offered. "We have to report to Mrs. Ripple anyway."

In the kitchen Mrs. Ripple was preparing supper. "For me?" she asked with surprise as Jeanmarie handed her the letter. "Can you stir this soup a moment, while I take a look?"

Jeanmarie took the long-handled spoon and began stirring the thick vegetable soup.

Mrs. Ripple stood next to her and opened the letter, a single page. "Oh!" she exclaimed. Her voice sounded so much like a cry that Jeanmarie nearly dropped the spoon. Mrs. Ripple's face had turned white.

"Bad news?" Jeanmarie said, forgetting to stir the pot.

"It's nothing. No. Nothing really." Mrs. Ripple thrust the letter into her apron pocket. Without a word she took the spoon from Jeanmarie and began stirring the soup hard. A moment later she shooed Jeanmarie away. "Do go on and leave me to my cooking, please."

Slowly Jeanmarie made her way upstairs. It wasn't like Mrs. Ripple to be brusque. Something in the letter had made her cry out. At the top of the stairs a flash of red caught Jeanmarie's eye—the new girl slipping into the doorway of the small dorm. What was she up to, and where was Winnie, who should have been watching her?

By supper time both the kitchen and the dining room smelled of the unmistakable odor of burnt food. Next to Jeanmarie, Pearl whispered, "How could anyone burn soup?"

"I don't know," Jeanmarie replied in a low voice. But Mrs. Ripple had managed, and from the look of the pudding she'd also burnt it. Something in that letter had upset Mrs. Ripple; but what? And the girls were none the wiser about their thief either. An upset stomach had forced Winnie to give up following Sophie. Across the room the new girl sent a quick look Jeanmarie's way. Did she know they were following her? If she did she was probably laughing inside while poor Winnie lay upstairs too sick to come to supper. Jeanmarie picked up her spoon and put it down again. Not that this meal would have helped Winnie or anyone else.

THREE

Broken Nests

Jeanmarie lingered on the last stone step of the administration building looking into the distance at the figure of Sophie on the girls' hill heading toward Wheelock. The bell signaling the end of the school day also sent everyone old enough to work to their assigned jobs. It couldn't be better for Sophie. Helping Mrs. Ripple in the house meant there were times when the little girls played in the yard and Mrs. Ripple was busy—time alone for Sophie with no one watching.

"Sophie working at Wheelock is like giving a fox the key to the chicken house. We'll never catch her in the act," Jeanmarie said, turning to Pearl, who stood waiting with an open book in her hands. "It all started when she came, and things are still disappearing. Half the checkers from the game so no one can play it now, the lace fringe Winnie was saving, buttons. Even the

27

needle and thread I left out to use yesterday were gone last night. It's a deliberate attempt to make the rest of us miserable, I think."

Closing her book, Pearl looked thoughtful. "Maybe we'd better talk to Mrs. Ripple." Pearl began walking and Jeanmarie joined her.

"What about Dr. Werner?" Jeanmarie reminded her. "And even if Mrs. Ripple doesn't call him in, what can she do? We have no proof."

Pearl shifted the book under her arm. "What if Sophie isn't guilty? It could be Leah. Or someone we haven't thought of yet," she added halfheartedly.

Jeanmarie stared at her friend. "You still don't think it's Sophie, do you? Why is everyone so ready to blame Leah?" Warmth flooded Jeanmarie's face. Here she was defending Leah, who a year ago she would have counted one of her worst enemies along with Leah's buddy, Emma. "Sorry," she said, gripping Pearl's arm. "But I think Leah's changed now that she's not under Emma's thumb anymore. She's good with the little girls in her dorm, and they like her. I can't help feeling that Sophie's the one."

Pearl shook her head. "Okay, but what about the list? Leah's on it too."

Jeanmarie didn't say what she was thinking. All the stories about Sophie's war hero parents didn't match up. Sophie had to be lying no matter how hard Pearl and the others tried to make excuses for the differences. If she lied about her folks, why couldn't she also be a thief? They were almost at the farmhouse, and once again Jeanmarie was late for work.

"Spring cleaning, right?" Pearl said and sighed. "Lucky for me Miss Riley makes the boys at Roth Cottage do all the hard stuff like washing walls. I don't mind doing kitchen cupboards and the pantry." She looked sympathetically at Jeanmarie. "I guess it's a lot better than what you'll be doing."

Jeanmarie took a deep breath. No one in the orphanage wanted to work at the farmhouse. "At least I know what to expect," she said. Short, stout Mrs. Koppel ran the farmhouse, which lodged staff, with the energy of a small locomotive. From the time Jeanmarie and her coworker, Gracie, arrived for work until they left, Mrs. Koppel rushed about determined to keep everything going at full speed, including the girls assigned to work for her. The farmhouse was already in sight, and Jeanmarie sighed. "See you tonight," she said to Pearl as she headed for the kitchen door.

Mrs. Koppel's voice carried from the dining room into the hallway. "Today you wash woodwork, scrub the floor, wax and polish the furniture." Jeanmarie peeked into the doorway where a red-faced Mrs. Koppel stood giving directions to Gracie, who had wound her blonde braids tightly around her head and wore an old white apron of Mrs. Koppel's. As usual Gracie had managed to arrive before Jeanmarie even though she lived in Ford Cottage north of Wheelock.

Mrs. Koppel glared at Jeanmarie. "Ach, always this von is late." She raised her stout arms in the air. "Such a ting! I should cook and clean and look after you two? Do I have time? No!" Handing Jeanmarie a large apron she pointed to the waiting pail of water and rags. Jeanmarie had barely slipped the apron on when Mrs. Koppel's strong arms propelled her into the room. Gracie looked at her and grinned. Jeanmarie swallowed hard. The two of them would have to race to get everything done before the evening meal.

The spring day had turned cloudy by the time Jeanmarie made her way back to the cottage. Her hands stung from ammonia water and her empty stomach rumbled.

A lone figure waited on the cottage steps. It was Maria; Jeanmarie knew by the mole on her face. Maria was holding out an envelope. "It's another letter for Mrs. Ripple. Like the last one, there's no return address. Thought you'd be coming along, so I waited," she said. "Dr. Werner came home just as I was finishing the vacuuming for Mrs. Werner and asked me to deliver it."

Jeanmarie looked at the letter closely. "This is the second one this week," she exclaimed. She studied the envelope. "Same printing too."

Maria took the letter back and held it on her palm. "Strange, isn't it? And so far, when she gets one of these, it's like whatever's in it has some power over her. From the look on her face, I'd say the letter she got two days ago made her angry. She didn't open it, just seemed to know who it came from."

Jeanmarie's stomach growled loudly. "That reminds me. We still have to give this to her, and there's no telling what she might do. Let's hope we're not having potato pancakes tonight unless you like them black."

"Oh no," Maria cried. "Please let it be something already in the oven."

Jeanmarie touched the letter Maria held, then drew her hand back quickly at a sudden thought. "A poison pen letter? Do you think the thief is writing these too?"

"Why would the thief do that?" Maria said.

Jeanmarie's thoughts whirled. "Whoever's stealing can't use all the things they take, and they know it's all stuff none of us can afford to lose, so why would they do it except for meanness? The letters could be another way to get at all of us through Mrs. Ripple." In her mind she thought "Sophie" though she'd said "whoever."

"You mean, if it's Sophie, she's taking out her anger on the rest of us orphans and Mrs. Ripple because she's the house-mother?" Maria sounded amazed.

"It's not impossible. We know someone is writing Mrs. Ripple letters, and they just have to be bad ones." Jeanmarie frowned. They had to find out, but how?

Mrs. Ripple was in the kitchen sipping a cup of tea. A deep flush rose in her face as she glanced at the letter Maria held out to her. "Thank you," was all she said, and she stuck the envelope into her apron pocket. Jeanmarie shrugged her shoulders lightly as Maria looked at her with raised eyebrows. From the table where she was piling slices of bread on platters, Sophie gave them a cold, searching look. Jeanmarie wondered, did she already know the contents of Mrs. Ripple's letter?

On Friday Pearl complained of a sore throat. By Saturday it seemed worse, and Mrs. Ripple ordered her to stay in bed. Jeanmarie left for work alone. The woods at the sides of the road looked greener and fuller to her, the leaves of the trees already unfurled since a week ago.

A red cardinal chirped loudly on a low maple branch, then flew out of sight. Close by, a brazen robin sang boldly, warning off intruders. Jeanmarie listened and gave him back a whistle. Though she had come to the orphanage from the city, she'd learned to see woods and trees and living things like birds and small animals in a new way. She could identify trees by their shapes, knew which birds made which sounds, and knew which wild plants to look for in spring. It gave her a good feeling. She supposed that's what God meant them all for.

Mrs. Shapiro greeted her with murmurs of sympathy for poor Pearl. "Such a shame," she said. "When you go you must take her some soft rolls, and help yourself, my dear. And today you must not try to do all the work alone. We will let the vacuuming go."

With a big apron tied about her waist Jeanmarie went to work on the dishes, scraping off remnants of noodles, meat, and gravy before rinsing them in the large sink. Mrs. Shapiro's friend was visiting again, and the two had gone out on the porch. The boy was nowhere in sight.

Jeanmarie worked hard and was almost finished with the kitchen when she dropped the rag she'd used to wipe the oil-cloth table cover. Bending to pick it up, she drew in her breath sharply as two brown shoes kicked out from under the table cover. Half crouching and crawling the boy emerged, ducked away from her, and ran out onto the porch. Jeanmarie stared after him. How long had he been under there watching her? It gave her an eerie feeling. He ought to have a friend to play with, she thought.

She'd mopped half the floor when her mop got tangled in something that scraped along the boards under the table. At first she thought it was a toy the boy must have been playing with, but as she held it up she noticed its gleaming shape was clear—a six-pointed star. Carefully she dried it off and placed it on the table where the boy would easily spot it. For the next hour she worked quickly, doing her own and as much of Pearl's work as she could.

Like a mother hen Mrs. Shapiro had insisted Jeanmarie take home a bag of rolls as well as an extra quarter along with her usual wage. With money clinking in her pocket and the bag of rolls in her hand, Jeanmarie walked slowly on the cottage path flanked by early yellow crocuses and purple hyacinth. She had gone only a few feet down the road to the orphanage when just ahead she saw Ralph, his tall, lanky frame leaning into a large bush; he was peering into the tangle of leafy branches he was holding apart. Turning his head he saw her and called, "You sure don't want to see this."

But Jeanmarie did. The angry red in Ralph's face and the turned-down look about his mouth as she approached should have warned her. She did not see the little thing on the ground until Ralph stooped down and scooped up a small baby sparrow in his hands. The tiny bird chirped weakly as she bent to look at it. "What happened to it?" she asked, reaching out to hold it.

"Fell when the nest broke," Ralph said. "I think he's got a broken wing, and someone or something has gone and smashed his nest. You can see the pieces in there." He pointed to the bush. "And it's not the only one either. There are two other nests like it. I found the first nest a few minutes ago in the woods back toward that cottage." He pointed in the direction of Mrs. Shapiro's. "They weren't all sparrow's nests. The broken eggs in the other nests were blue—robin's eggs." He touched the feathered head of the baby sparrow lightly. "This little fellow was the only one that survived, though his home didn't."

Ralph held the branches of the bush apart for Jeanmarie to look. Inside, still stuck among the branches, were broken pieces of nest, its intricately woven grasses torn apart. Parts of the nest lay on the ground near two tiny dead sparrows. "It looks like someone used a heavy club or stick to smash into the nest, and these little fellows were thrown out," Ralph said. Two other small birds lay on the ground, unmoving.

Jeanmarie stroked the tiny thing in her hand. "Will he live?" she asked. "We can't just leave him here, poor thing."

"I think we can fix up that wing. If we leave him here he'll die for sure. I'll take him home, feed him, try a splint on that wing, and we'll see," Ralph said, taking the bird from her. "He must have been the strongest of the bunch from the size of him. Now what I need is something to carry him in."

"What about my paper bag?" Jeanmarie offered. Quickly she stuffed the rolls into her pockets and turned down the edges of the bag to make a nest for the baby bird. "With a little soft grass in the bottom it ought to do until you get him home." Ralph transferred the baby bird into the improvised nest where it complained loudly and fluttered its good wing.

As the two walked Jeanmarie tried to imagine what might have happened to the nests. She hardly dared to ask but managed, "How many baby birds were there?"

"This one was the only nest with baby birds in it, but the other two had eggs that will never hatch now. One thing's sure; none of those nests fell out of trees. They were all nests built in bushes and all of them just torn apart."

"Could some animal have done it?" Jeanmarie asked.

He shook his head. "If it was an animal it would have eaten the eggs and probably the babies too. Animals don't usually tear up nests like that and knock them to the ground for no reason."

Jeanmarie felt angry. If an animal didn't do it, who did? She looked at the stretch of woods near the cottage. It was the kind of cruel thing a bully might do, but it made no sense. "I can't imagine who could have done it," she said. "The only cottage close by is the Shapiros' where I work. They don't even have children." She didn't bother to mention the boy who never said a word and ran like a scared little rabbit when anyone looked at him. Besides, he didn't live there anyway.

"Might be some mean tramp just passing through," Ralph said. "Whoever it is better hope I never catch him doing such a thing."

"Do you come here to hunt often?" Jeanmarie asked. "I notice you don't have your rifle today." The week before when she and Pearl had seen him in the woods he'd had his rifle with him.

Red again colored Ralph's face. "Didn't bring it today. You always work on Saturday?"

Jeanmarie nodded. "Usually it's the two of us, but Pearl had a sore throat and couldn't come."

"In that case I'll walk on back with you," Ralph said, avoiding her eyes.

The baby sparrow chirped and fluttered in his bag nest. Jeanmarie reached out her hands. "Is it okay if I carry him?" she asked.

FOUR

A Game
of Charades

Sunday morning a steady rain fell in thin slant lines like fine brush strokes against the trees and meadow. Jeanmarie plopped her rain hat on as she hurried down to the church. The large stone building that housed the orphanage school, chapel, and staff offices looked dark and more forbidding than usual under the gray sky. The rest of the choir girls were already entering the school entrance as Jeanmarie hung her wet raincoat in the cloakroom. In the corner, on the last hanger, her black robe and cap waited next to the white starched surplice with the great full sleeves that always made her feel like a bird ready to take off. She dressed quickly in the girls' room. With a final glance in the mirror she patted the round black cap into place on the back of her head, pinned it with a precious bobby pin, her last, and hurried to join the others.

The new chaplain, an elderly man with white hair and a round cheerful face, smiled as the girls filed into the choir pews. Jeanmarie smiled back. She liked the old man. His kind voice and frequent laughter made it easy to listen to him, when she wasn't thinking of something else. She meant to listen, but it was hard having to look at all those faces in front of the choir stalls. A warm feeling flooded her face as her eyes met those of the tall boy in the last row. It was Ralph; he was wearing a white shirt, and his dark shiny hair was slicked smooth. The chaplain was saying something about sparrows when she turned her eyes away.

"So, my dear children, always remember that our heavenly Father sees every sparrow who falls to the ground and that each of you is much more valuable than a sparrow." Once more Jeanmarie's thoughts wandered, this time back to the baby sparrow Ralph had found. Had it survived the night? She glanced in Ralph's direction and saw him smile broadly at her. Did he mean to let her know that the sparrow was okay?

After church Jeanmarie looked for Ralph, but the new farmer and his thin little wife were already leaving with Ralph walking between them. He didn't look back as Jeanmarie turned toward Wheelock Cottage.

Beside her Winnie struggled with an old umbrella. "This thing isn't worth the trouble it takes to keep it up," she muttered. Rain ran down Winnie's face, and her wet hair lay flat against her head.

"Win, you'll catch cold for sure," Pearl said, trying to unstick the bent umbrella spokes. As if in agreement Winnie sneezed. "At least take my rain hat while I work on this thing," Pearl offered.

"Neither one of you ought to be getting soaked. Pearl, you're just getting over a sore throat, and Winnie, you know you have to be careful," Jeanmarie said undoing her own rain hat. "I don't need this, so please put it on, Win."

"Thanks," Winnie said, taking the hat and putting it on. "I looked everywhere for my hat and just couldn't find it."

"Don't tell me our thief is taking rain hats now," Jeanmarie said. "Though why not? What kind of thief takes bobby pins or any of the other stuff we're missing?" Halfway up the hill ahead of them she saw Sophie walking alone, her head bent against the rain, her red hair sleek with water. It had to be her! At least she wasn't bold enough to wear Winnie's hat. Anger flipped Jeanmarie's insides.

Pearl gave the half-open umbrella back to Winnie, who held it above them. "I've been thinking," Pearl said slowly. "What worries me is that we don't know what else Mrs. Ripple might be missing besides her scissors and change purse. And if it is something valuable, what's to say it can't happen to us? If the dorm isn't safe anymore, where do we put things?"

Jeanmarie thought of Pearl's prize possession—the small silver cross her aunt had sent her before she died, her only tie to the family Pearl had never known. And what about her own keepsakes? She thought of the carved bird on a leather necklace in the box she kept by her bed. She meant to keep it forever, and no thief had better steal it.

It was neither Pearl nor Jeanmarie who sent a loud wail through the dorm just after lunch. "My charm bracelet," Maria cried. "It's gone!" A search of dresser drawers, closet, floor, and every possible place proved fruitless. Tears of anger ran down Maria's face. "I've always had that bracelet; a silver fish, a tiny cross, a little book, and a carved rose on it. I can't lose it," Maria wailed.

"That does it," Jeanmarie stated. A plan already forming in her head, she beckoned the others away from the door where they might be overheard. "We haven't looked in the small dorm yet. We can start there. Maybe we'll find something, maybe not. What if we search Sophie's things while she's out? I know it's risky, but tonight after supper two of us could slip out while everyone's in the game room. One can keep watch while the other searches. I'll be glad to be one of the two."

Pearl quickly volunteered. "I'll help so we can get on with the list."

Jeanmarie didn't look at her. "Okay then. We'll do it."

"We'll have to keep Sophie downstairs while you're up there," Winnie said, shaking her head.

"If anyone can, it's you, Win," Jeanmarie said and smiled. Winnie, with her soft, motherly ways, was their best bet. "Then it's settled. If we have to go through every dresser drawer and closet corner we will." Maria's charm bracelet was just the evidence they needed. Jeanmarie pictured the bracelet lying hidden in Sophie's drawer. She wasn't so sure Sophie would admit anything even then, but the evidence would be proof enough.

A light rapping at the partially closed door made the girls turn. "May I come in?" Mrs. Ripple, wearing a white apron over her blue flowered dress, stood framed in the doorway. Her hair in thick gold braids around her head gleamed as if freshly washed, and her smile said that this was a friendly call. "I won't keep you but a minute. I've something I'd like to tell you that might just be fun for everyone." In a moment she had seated herself on the edge of Jeanmarie's cot. Keeping her voice low as if she were about to share something secretive, she said, "All of you have probably noticed that our new girl, Sophie, seems to be having some difficulty adjusting to being here with us. I suppose some of you remember your first days in the orphanage and how strange everything seemed in your new surroundings?"

Jeanmarie stared at her. Did she know about the girl's thieving? But what did being new have to do with it?

Mrs. Ripple smiled and went on. "I would like all of us to make an even greater effort to help her feel welcome here. I've decided that tonight we must have an ice-cream party. In fact I made the ice cream this morning with Leah to help crank, and it looks just fine. Afterwards we can choose teams and play charades. That way we can include Sophie and let her get to know us a little more. Besides, charades have always been a favorite of mine. Now I must see to supper, but I'll be counting on each of you to help make tonight fun for all of us, including Sophie. Well, what do you think?"

Winnie smiled sweetly. "It's a great idea. Who can resist ice cream?"

"I'll take it that Winnie speaks for all of you?" asked Mrs. Ripple. Pearl and the twins nodded as Jeanmarie too gave a halfhearted nod. "Good. I'll look for each of you to do your part tonight," she said. In silence the girls watched her leave.

Sniffling, Winnie looked relieved. "I guess that puts an end to the search for tonight. We'll all be downstairs trying to help Sophie feel at home."

Pearl shrugged her shoulders. "Mrs. Ripple has no reason to think Sophie might have her change purse and her scissors and whatever else she's missing, or that she could be the one behind the letters." Jeanmarie bit her lip when Pearl said "Sophie might have." *Am I the only one who really thinks Sophie is the thief?*, she thought.

Jeanmarie frowned. Mrs. Ripple had only made it harder for them to find the evidence they needed. None of them could leave the teams if they played charades, but maybe there was a way. "I think we can still search Sophie's things," she said. "While everyone is eating ice cream, I can excuse myself to go upstairs to the bathroom. The rest of you stall for time and make sure Sophie doesn't follow me."

The party had started when Jeanmarie excused herself and slipped out. The small dormitory where Leah, the younger girls, and Sophie slept looked much like the larger dormitory with its iron cots. In the far corner stood the dresser. One of the drawers belonged to Sophie, but which one? As quietly as she could, Jeanmarie opened the top drawer. From the size of the small socks lying on top of a pile she knew at once that it belonged to one of the little girls. She closed it quickly just as the phone in the hallway rang loudly. Panic struck her. Mrs. Ripple would answer it any moment. She flew to the door, but there was no time; footsteps were already coming up the stairs and in a hurry. Hardly daring to breathe, Jeanmarie flattened herself against the wall behind the dormitory door and listened.

"Hello, Mrs. Ripple here." The housemother's next words sent a shiver through Jeanmarie. The sharpness in her voice rose. "Oh, Hattie, there's been another letter. I don't know what to do. If only your father was alive to help." For the next few minutes Jeanmarie heard nothing as Mrs. Ripple must have been listening to someone named Hattie on the other end. Finally she said, "Thank you. Don't worry about me. I'll be alright. I have a job to do here, and I must just put other things out of my mind. . . . Yes, that's true. . . . I'd better go back to the girls. We're about to play charades. . . . Yes, maybe it will take my mind off this for now."

Jeanmarie waited until she was sure Mrs. Ripple had gone downstairs. What was in those terrible letters to upset her so? If only there was some way to see inside them. And how could Hattie's father have helped if he was alive? Did she mean he would know what to do about the poison pen letters? It was all like a giant real-life charades waiting to be solved. Jeanmarie glanced longingly at the dresser, but she didn't dare take any longer. The game of charades would be starting downstairs any second. The search would have to wait, or someone might come looking for her.

FIVE

A Small Taped Box

Morning came clear and cool with a spring sun not yet strong enough for warmth. Throwing on her jacket Jeanmarie hurried from the cellar door, knowing she was already late for work at the farmhouse. Her stomach rumbled hungrily, reminding her that breakfast depended on Mrs. Koppel not noticing the clock.

Mrs. Koppel *did* notice. Jeanmarie's punishment as usual had been no breakfast. She tried not to think of food as she put away the dust mop, emptied the last wastebasket, and left for school. Gracie, already finished, stood outside waiting. She shook her head when Jeanmarie caught up. "You can't keep skipping breakfast and eating half your lunch before school. You're skinny enough now."

Jeanmarie took her sandwich from her lunch bag. "It's one of my faults," she admitted. "Potted meat again," she said, examining the contents between the slices of bread. "And late means no time for breakfast. It's Mrs. Koppel's idea of a right punishment. Don't worry about me, Gracie. I'll make up for it at supper." *Unless,* she thought, *Mrs. Ripple burns it again.* Lately, the housemother's mind didn't seem to be on cooking.

Inside the classroom the morning clatter and chatter of voices stopped as Mrs. Gillpin rapped sharply on her desk. Jeanmarie slid quickly into her seat and slipped her half-eaten lunch into the desk. From the seat ahead of her Pearl turned slightly to whisper, "Thought you might want the extra bread in your desk."

"Thanks," Jeanmarie whispered back. She felt for the bread, found it wrapped in a napkin, and stuffed it into the paper bag. It was just like Pearl to know she'd need it. The bread would add to her small lunch at noon. Mrs. Gillpin had opened the large black Bible and begun reading. Jeanmarie listened to the words of the psalm: "In thee, O LORD, do I put my trust: let me never be put to confusion."

But by midafternoon Jeanmarie felt something very like confusion mixed with anger and things she didn't want to name. Mrs. Gillpin handed back first their math tests, and then the social studies test. Her look of delight and cheerful voice were directed straight at Sophie. "I want you all to know, class, that our newest student, Sophie, has once again showed her ability by a perfect math score and a perfect social studies test." Cries of "Wow!" and "Not again!" sounded around the classroom.

Jeanmarie looked at Wilfred. Up until now, he had been the class brain. His scores were high as usual but not perfect. He glanced at the papers Mrs. Gillpin handed him along with her praise for a good job done, pushed his glasses back on his nose, and looked up with a broad grin. The smile was for Sophie, who sat directly across from him, a half-smile on her face. Jeanmarie shook her head. Didn't Wilfred know that Sophie's smile was one of triumph?

"Now, class," Mrs. Gillpin said, drawing their attention, "I want you to choose a partner for your art projects. You know your projects will be judged and are due next Friday. You and your partner will have time to plan today and work together during art period for the rest of this week and next. I suspect most of you have already discussed this since you've known about it for a while, so now you may quietly begin." In a moment almost everyone was exchanging seats to sit near a friend. Jeanmarie moved over as Pearl slid in next to her.

Across the room Sophie remained at her desk, alone. But as Jeanmarie and Pearl watched, Wilfred pushed his desk close to Sophie's. The two of them were already at work drawing something on a piece of paper when Jeanmarie looked away. Wilfred had deliberately chosen Sophie. He could have partnered with any of the boys, who were always eager to have Wilfred do most of the work, but he'd chosen Sophie. If only he knew who was really sitting next to him!

Pearl whispered in a low voice, "At least he won't have to do all the thinking this time." Jeanmarie didn't answer. Sophie might be smart, but that only made her a clever thief. Jeanmarie tried to concentrate on the paper Pearl pushed toward her, but all she could think of was Wilfred. He'd stuck by her in some of her worst times at the orphanage, and it made her angry to see Sophie take over. But of course he didn't know the truth about her, not yet.

Absentmindedly, Jeanmarie drew a small dog on the corner of the paper nearest her. Did Sophie like dogs? she wondered. She had better, since every stray dog around loved Wilfred, and one or another of them was always following him.

Pearl turned the paper toward her and grinned. "Dogs—a great idea. We could do a parade, all sizes, shapes, kinds. Or how about doggy wallpaper designs?"

Jeanmarie grinned back. "That's not a bad idea; I mean the wallpaper." For a while both girls concentrated on the work in front of them. Once Jeanmarie glanced over at Wilfred and Sophie. The two seemed totally involved in their project planning. The afternoon went quickly, and before she knew it school was out and Wilfred had disappeared to the boys' hill. She had no idea what she planned to say to him, but it would have to wait anyway.

When her work at the farmhouse ended, Jeanmarie could hardly wait for supper, thanks to her small lunch and no breakfast. Tired, and smelling of the ammonia water she and Gracie had used to wash the hall walls, she hurried home thinking of one thing—food.

Tess stood waiting at the edge of the path where the road wound past Wheelock. "You won't believe it!" she cried. "I did it. My work ended early today, so when I came home and Mrs. Ripple and Sophie were busy in the kitchen, I just took a chance and went upstairs to look around."

Jeanmarie stared at her. "You searched Sophie's things?"

Tess nodded. "Somebody had to do it. I went in, and no one was there, so I looked for her dresser drawer. I found it; I knew it was hers, because she has that yellow sweater with the white trim, and it was in there." Tess's dark eyes were serious. "I felt a lump under the sweater and found a small heavily taped box, nothing else. Course, I didn't dare open the box. We don't have any proof that Sophie's guilty. Maybe she keeps something she treasures in the box. That's all I saw."

"Nothing else?" Jeanmarie insisted. "None of the missing stuff, stamps or anything?"

"Just the box and her clothes. I'm not convinced Sophie's the one we're looking for," Tess added softly.

Jeanmarie frowned. "Who else could it be? She might have hidden stuff someplace else, all except the box. The big problem is, how do we find out what's in the box?" It could be the evidence they needed. Aloud she said, "It must be something pretty valuable, if she has it all tightly taped up like that." At least they were getting closer to some real proof. Her stomach reminded her that she didn't want to miss another meal. "We'd better hurry or we'll be late for supper," she said, quickening her steps.

"Wait; there's one other thing you need to know," Tess said. "I saw Emma today with Leah. It looked a lot like the old days the way they had their heads together. My guess is Leah's our thief, and maybe Emma put her up to it."

Jeanmarie swallowed hard. "I can't believe Leah would steal from me, us, I mean. She really has changed even if Emma hasn't. If Emma still wants to hang around with Leah that doesn't mean Leah wants it too. Just talking to someone isn't proof she's the thief, is it?" Jeanmarie heard herself defending Leah again. But what if it was Leah? What about Sophie? "Sophie's the one; you'll see, once we find out what's in that box. It might even be Maria's charm bracelet."

Tess pressed her lips together and didn't say a word. Jeanmarie turned away, determined to look inside that box and soon.

The supper bell hadn't rung yet. Tess went to find Maria, and Jeanmarie ran upstairs to the washroom. She was just in time to hear Mrs. Ripple saying to someone on the other end of the hallway phone, "No. I tell you I don't have it right now." Jeanmarie tiptoed past Mrs. Ripple, whose back was to her, slipped into the washroom, and shut the door. She thought of leaving it open but didn't dare. What was missing? And who wanted it back? Could Sophie have taken whatever it was? Maybe that was what was in the heavily taped box.

Across the hall, the door shut tightly behind her, Sophie opened her dresser drawer and reached for the yellow sweater. As she lifted it a small heavily taped box rolled over. For a moment she stared at the box, then let her fingers close tightly around it. She wanted so much to tear off the tape, but she mustn't. Instead, she pushed the box deeper into the drawer, put on the sweater, and left.

SIX

A Near Accident

S orry," Pearl said. "I hate to miss work again, but it's the only time the dentist can take me." The left side of her face looked swollen, and she sounded as if it hurt to talk. As if to affirm that it did hurt, she gingerly touched the area and yelped.

Jeanmarie winced. "At least you don't have to wait until Monday," she said. The trip to the dentist's office generally took thirty minutes each way, but rarely did anyone from the orphanage go except for emergencies. Thankfully, Jeanmarie had only made the trip once, and that was for a cracked tooth. "I don't think you could work the way that jaw looks." Sympathy for Pearl filled her as Pearl gingerly tried to smile. "Why don't you try a hot towel on it?" Jeanmarie suggested. Barely moving her head, Pearl nodded.

In the hallway Jeanmarie nearly collided with Lizzie, whose small arms were wound around a large bowl of water. Behind her May followed, carefully holding a bottle of witch hazel. "Whoa there, young ladies. Where are you off to with the hazel water?" Jeanmarie said, steadying the bowl in Lizzie's arms.

"It's for Leah," May exclaimed. "She's got poison ivy real bad." Lizzie nodded her head in agreement.

"Leah?" Jeanmarie hadn't seen the girl in two days. "Why don't I just carry the bowl in for you, Lizzie, and that way I can make a quick visit to Leah too."

"Nope," the small girl said, shaking her head. "Got to do it by myself. I won't spill it if you don't go bumping me again, Jeanmarie-Nanny," she promised, then grinned.

Jeanmarie smiled back and flicked a stubborn lock of hair from Lizzie's forehead. "Looks like you have everything under control. You carry the bowl, and I'll just tag along for a minute." First Pearl, now Leah. In the orphanage, sickness came often.

On her cot propped against a pile of pillows, Leah looked awful. An angry red rash covered both sides of her face, but it was her hands that made Jeanmarie gasp. Leah's arms lay flat against the sheet on both sides of her, the fingers swollen like sausages. Between each finger, blisters, some the size of giant marbles, spread her fingers wide apart. It was obvious she could do nothing with her hands. As Jeanmarie leaned closer Leah sighed. "Poison ivy," she said. "Never had it so bad before."

Lizzie set the bowl on the stand next to the bed and stepped back for May, who poured in the witch hazel. "We're Leah's nurses. Mrs. Ripple said we could," Lizzie explained as she swished two white cloths in the bowl. "We keep the water cool and put in fresh medicine." Carefully she wrung out one cloth and handed it to May, who took it to the other side of the cot and draped it over the right side of Leah's face. Lizzie did the same with hers on the left side. The two proceeded to repeat the operation, this time draping the cool cloths over each of Leah's hands. "Feel better?" Lizzie asked. Leah nodded.

"I'm really sorry, Leah," Jeanmarie said. "If you need anything I'd be glad to help."

Lizzie frowned, and Jeanmarie quickly added, "With these two nurses on duty you're in good hands, and I have to go to work, but I promise I'll pop in again after work." Leah nodded.

On her way out Jeanmarie stopped at the kitchen to report to Mrs. Ripple. "I'm leaving for off-grounds work," she called from the doorway. "Oh," she added, "Lizzie and May are handling nursing Leah really well."

From the kitchen sink where she'd been bending over a wet mound of potatoes, Mrs. Ripple raised a pale face to Jeanmarie. Dark circles shadowed her eyes as if she hadn't slept well. "Thank you," she said. "I'd nearly forgotten poor Leah's wet cloths. Maybe we could put a bit of ice into the bowl for her. You run along. I'll see to it." She turned away, her tall frame bending once more over the sink.

Jeanmarie frowned as she left. Whatever was bothering Mrs. Ripple clearly hadn't gone away. First the letters, then the phone calls; no wonder she looked worn out. Strange too, that no one seemed to be missing anything for the last three days. Either Sophie hadn't found time to steal lately or she knew they were watching her and was laying low. "At least we know who our thief is," Jeanmarie whispered to herself. The box and whatever was in it would be all the proof they needed.

The woods on either side of the road to the Shapiros' cottage were no longer thin stands of bare trees Jeanmarie could look through. Every tree and bush swelled with newly grown leaves and filled the empty spaces, shutting in the forest from prying eyes. The day felt warm, and Jeanmarie pushed a loose strand of hair behind her ear. It was the perfect day for a long hike in the woods. The faint sweet smell of some flowering bush nearby wafted toward her, and she sighed. This was a workday. Ahead of her the Shapiros' cottage came into sight.

Mrs. Shapiro's kind face looked sympathetic when Jeanmarie explained about Pearl's toothache. "Such a thing," she exclaimed in a grandmotherly voice. "Always you should have cloves for pain. 'Cloves for the teeth,' my great-aunt Miriam always said, rest her soul." Jeanmarie thought to herself, with a jaw like Pearl's, not even Aunt Miriam's cloves would help. Mrs. Shapiro patted Jeanmarie's head and led her into the kitchen. Dirty dishes lay piled high. "So, you do your best, eh? The dishes, a light dusting, and quick mopping—who could ask for more?" The usual tray of cookies sat waiting on the table. Mrs. Shapiro smiled at Jeanmarie. "And you help yourself for you and your friend, eh?"

Jeanmarie swished hot soapy water over a plate. Mrs. Shapiro was nice. No long list of special instructions; she just expected you to do the work and left it to you. Jeanmarie liked that. It made her feel trusted. Mrs. Shapiro would have made a good housemother. Her thoughts went to Mrs. Ripple. If only there was some way to help her.

A footstep behind her made her turn quickly. The dark-haired boy stood near the table, a cookie in his hand. "Mrs. Shapiro said I could have one," he said. He held the cookie partway to his mouth as if waiting for permission to eat it.

This was the first time Jeanmarie had heard the boy say anything. "Sounds good to me," she replied and smiled. "In fact, if you don't mind I'd like one myself. Mrs. Shapiro said I could have some too," she added quickly. The boy nodded solemnly and bit into the chocolate cookie.

Jeanmarie wiped her hands on her apron. Fearing to startle him, she moved slowly, chose a small cookie, and bit into it. "Great," she said. "I guess you and your grandma have these often when you come for visits. I've seen you here before. It's a great place for a cottage. My name's Jeanmarie. What's yours?"

"David," the boy said. "How come you work here?" he asked. "Mrs. Shapiro says you live in an orphanage up the road." He helped himself to another cookie and stood eating and looking at Jeanmarie, his dark eyes made even darker by his pale skin.

Jeanmarie wondered if he was sickly. She explained about the orphanage and off-ground jobs. "My friend Pearl couldn't make it today thanks to a bad toothache," she added.

"Saw her and you and that big boy the other day in the woods," David said. For a moment he looked uneasy. "Big boys with guns oughtn't be coming around here. I don't like guns. Didn't see him today."

"Ralph? He wouldn't hurt anyone. That's just his hunting rifle, and he only uses it for practice, I'm certain. Don't worry about him. You might want to watch out for tramps. Some mean old tramp destroyed a bunch of birds' nests not far from here. I'd look out for him." As soon as the words were out she wished she'd never said them.

The boy's face went even whiter than it had been. His eyes grew wide. He turned away quickly. "Got to go." He was gone before Jeanmarie could say anything more. She should have known better. He was just a little boy, and on top of that, he seemed so nervous, maybe sickly.

At 4:00 Jeanmarie left, carrying a full sack of cookies for Pearl. The boy was nowhere in sight. Was he hiding from her now? Watching her from the woods? By the time she'd come to the end of the cottage path and walked a distance down the road her thoughts were no longer on the boy. Ralph, still dressed in work overalls, was striding toward her.

His grin made her forget that she was wearing her faded work dress and hadn't even stopped to redo a stubborn braid that slapped loosely against her shoulder. "Hi," he said. "Found a patch of violets today." In his hand was a small bunch of the deep purple flowers surrounded by soft green leaves. "You know, you can eat 'em with a little sugar or just stick 'em in a jar." Two patches of red stood out on his face as he held the flowers out to Jeanmarie. "Here."

Warmth flooded Jeanmarie's face. Looking down at the flowers, she took them carefully from his big hand. "Thanks. I never ate a violet before, but there's always a first time."

"That's what I like about the spring. A fellow could live outdoors, and if he knew enough, never go hungry."

A sudden thought came into Jeanmarie's head. "Like that tramp, the one who might have broken the bird nests?"

Ralph smiled at her. "Not likely. Tramps mostly don't stay in one place long enough. My pa says if a man's lazy enough to be a tramp, he won't bother trying to live off the land when he can just beg or steal instead. But my grandpa used to say that if a fellow respected the outdoors, with a little learning he could be right at home in any woods."

Jeanmarie nodded. She knew Ralph was that kind. "How's the sparrow doing?" she asked.

"Perky little thing," he said. "I think the splint is holding, and he's eating okay. Looks like he'll make it." The sound of a speeding truck coming from behind them made them both look back. The expression on Ralph's face was one of surprise and fear. "Look out!" he cried, pushing Jeanmarie to the side of the road and nearly falling himself as he leapt out of the way. The truck skidded to a stop almost on top of them.

Jeanmarie's heart pounded as she looked from Ralph to the pickup truck and its driver. The farmer! Ralph's father sat behind the wheel, a dark scowl on his large face.

He opened the side door and shouted at Ralph. "Just what do you think you're doing? Get in here now!" Without a word to Jeanmarie, Ralph climbed in beside his father. The farmer started up the truck almost before the door had slammed shut and sped away, weaving crazily down the road.

Stunned, Jeanmarie stood at the roadside. The man had almost run them down. And he'd acted as if Jeanmarie didn't even exist! She hadn't done anything, but she felt as guilty as though she and Ralph had been caught stealing or something. What had Ralph done to make his father so furious? She began walking almost blindly along the deserted road toward the orphanage. The sound of loud barking startled her. Just ahead at the edge of the woods a short-haired dog came bounding onto the road. Behind him came Wilfred. He waved merrily at her.

"You," she said as he joined her. "What are you doing here?" Her voice was sharp. The scene with Ralph and his father had left her angry. She bit her lip at the surprised look on Wilfred's face. It wasn't his fault.

"Officially I'm taking Gypsy here back to her rightful owner. For a minute I thought you and Ralph were goners and that maybe the truck had gone haywire. Then I saw Ralph's father pick up Ralph and speed away like he was mad at the world. And there you were in the middle of the road." Wilfred pushed his glasses back on his nose. "He's a good farmer and doesn't bother with the rest of us much. Saves his temper for his family mostly. He doesn't like his son hanging around with orphans," Wilfred said. The dog nosed its way close to Wilfred, then ran ahead a little and waited.

Jeanmarie stared at Wilfred. "How do you know that?" she demanded. Anger made her stomach churn as Wilfred explained how the farmer treated his work crew fairly but not in a friendly manner.

"Are you saying Ralph's father doesn't like orphans? Or just that he doesn't want his son to pick up any low-down orphan ways?" Her face burned as words she didn't even stop to think about spilled out.

Wilfred grinned. "Didn't say either one. Some people put a lot of stock into family backgrounds—where you come from, who your folks were, that kind of thing. The new farmer's that way. The boys on his crew know it. He doesn't allow his son to make friends with orphans."

"But that's the dumbest thing I ever heard," Jeanmarie wailed. "If that's so, then why does he let Ralph come to the gym Saturday nights?"

"You didn't know?" Wilfred said. "The farmer and his wife go to visit Ralph's grandparents way down in Little Falls. Some Saturday nights Ralph stays home to do his school-work. That's when he goes to the gym; they'd never let him go if they knew." They were at the path to Wheelock, and Wilfred turned to leave. "I'll see you. Don't take it too hard," he said. "Ralph's okay. It's just his dad."

Jeanmarie glared at Wilfred. "Who cares anyway," she said. "I'm not interested in what Ralph's father thinks about orphans." She didn't look back. She swiped at a tear on her cheek. Why should she cry when she was so angry? By the time she reached Wheelock she'd managed to calm down. She wouldn't tell anyone until she'd figured it out herself.

Pearl was waiting for her. "Oh no!" Jeanmarie said, looking at Pearl's still swollen face. "Brought you some great cookies." Jeanmarie held out the bag from Mrs. Shapiro. "You can save them for later. They'll still be good."

Pearl nodded. "It's not as bad as it looks," she said in a thin voice. Jeanmarie smiled. "Really," Pearl insisted. "The doctor drained it and gave me pills to take, and it feels better. I have to go back next week," she added.

"Oh." Jeanmarie hadn't expected that. It meant she'd have to go to the Shapiros' cottage by herself again. She swallowed hard. She wanted to tell Pearl that she'd nearly been run down this afternoon, but not yet.

She was still thinking about Wilfred's words long after lights-out. The picture of the farmer's angry face and the sound of the racing truck kept coming back to her. She must have fallen asleep and dreamed a huge black car was about to run her down when something woke her. Jeanmarie sat up, wide awake now. Quietly she pushed back the blanket, got up, and slipped past the others, who were still sleeping soundly, and walked into the hallway. She listened and then she heard it: muffled, whimpering sounds coming from the small dorm.

Jeanmarie stood in the doorway. The sounds were coming from the room where Leah slept. Leah, it must be her. As she neared Leah's cot she whispered, "It's me, Jeanmarie. Is it the poison ivy? Should I wake up Mrs. Ripple?"

"No; don't wake her up. I just need to take a pill and put the compresses back on. But every time I try, my fingers won't work right," Leah said. "There's a pill on the stand next to that glass, but I can't get hold of it."

Jeanmarie found the pill and held it along with the glass of water. "I'll slip it into your mouth and then you can drink this; good," she said as Leah managed to swallow both the pill and the water. The cloths on Leah's nightstand were barely damp, and what was left of the water in the bowl felt lukewarm to Jeanmarie's touch. "I need to get cool water and put in some fresh witch hazel, okay?" Leah whispered her thanks.

For the next few minutes Jeanmarie sat on the floor by Leah keeping the wet compresses on Leah's face and hands. Jeanmarie had begun yawning great yawns, and her eyes were beginning to burn. She pressed her lips together hard. She'd broken her promise to visit Leah after work and couldn't just leave her now.

Twice Jeanmarie refilled the bowl with cool water. Finally Leah whispered, "The medicine's helping. I think I can sleep now."

"If you're sure, I'll go on back to bed. I'll check on you in a couple of hours," Jeanmarie promised. This time she'd keep her promise. "Try to sleep," she urged. Her own eyelids kept closing as she stumbled back to bed. She hadn't realized the bottle of witch hazel was still in her hand; sleepily she put it next to her bed. It would be right there for when she checked on Leah. Already her eyes were closing. "Please, God, help Leah," she murmured. Had she said the words or only thought them? she wondered as the bed rose up to meet her.

Two hours later Jeanmarie sat up and once more made her way to Leah's bed. Leah was sound asleep. The cloths on Leah's hands felt cool and wet to Jeanmarie. Someone must have filled the bowl with fresh water. Next to it stood the bottle of witch hazel. Puzzled, Jeanmarie touched it, remembering she'd taken it with her last time. Mrs. Ripple must have come in, found it, and brought it back. A great yawn took her, and Jeanmarie headed for her own bed.

From under the corner of her blanket where she had been watching, Sophie smiled. Jeanmarie hadn't awakened at all when Sophie had taken the witch hazel bottle from her bedside to freshen Leah's compresses. It was all she could do for poor Leah. In some ways she and Leah were alike. Leah didn't seem to have any real friends or family either. Both of them were in the dorm with the youngest orphans, instead of with the others their age. It wasn't fair.

Back in bed Jeanmarie drew the blanket about her tightly. What if the nightmare came back? She shivered and tried not to think about it. Not even Ralph's father would do such a terrible thing like running her down. At least he wouldn't mean to, but with his terrible temper, what if he had?

SEVEN

The Stranger

"Please wake up." The voice was Pearl's. Jeanmarie opened her eyes. Pearl, dressed in her Sunday clothes, was leaning over her, an anxious look on her face. "Everyone's downstairs waiting for you; you better move fast."

"What's the matter?" Jeanmarie said, squinting at the clock on the wall. She hadn't heard a thing until just now. "It's late!" she exclaimed, yanking the bed cover up and plopping the still warm pillow on top. She pulled on her clothes and smoothed down her hair. Everything else would have to wait. "Hey, how are you feeling?" she asked Pearl.

"I could eat most anything this morning, I'm so hungry," Pearl replied.

"Starved is the word," Jeanmarie added, stifling a yawn as the two hurried downstairs. It had been a long night, and she felt she could eat double helpings of anything, except maybe burnt cereal. But surely Mrs. Ripple wouldn't let that happen again this morning. At least she wasn't facing Mrs. Koppel. So far she'd never been late for a meal under Mrs. Ripple. This was not the day to find out how strict she could be. With seconds to spare Jeanmarie slipped into her chair in the dining room as Pearl took hers. An unsmiling Mrs. Ripple nodded and began saying grace. "Thanks," Jeanmarie whispered. She meant for letting them be on time.

By Monday the art project was almost done. Jeanmarie came awake before any of the others were up. She lifted a corner of the blackout curtain and peered outside. Faint color streaked the sky as dawn spread its light. Quietly she shook Pearl. "Time," she whispered. The two dressed and tiptoed downstairs to the basement to make the final touches on their project.

Propped on a sack full of potatoes the roofless miniature room with its lace curtains made from an old handkerchief, its painted wallpaper, and the woven rug that had once been part of a knitted potholder needed only one last touch from Jeanmarie's thin paint brush. While Pearl held the paints Jeanmarie painted. "There," she said, filling in the last leaf of the tiny sprig of flowers on the little cardboard dresser. The canopy bed, held up by four white pencil posts, had two soft pillows Pearl had made from cotton balls pulled into squares and decorated with bits of pink ribbon. All in all the model Victorian room looked great. "Do you think we need a sign telling what book we copied the Victorian patterns from?" she asked.

Pearl blew softly on the freshly painted dresser. "We better make one. That way we can put our names on it too. How about attaching it to the bedroom door?"

The little room seemed almost enchanting, and Jeanmarie had to tear herself away for work. When at last she ran from the farmhouse slightly late for school, Pearl was already there with the project. The classroom display table held several finished projects. Pearl had placed theirs next to a shoe-box theater with miniature stick puppets in it. There were no other Victorian rooms.

Jeanmarie smiled broadly. Designing wallpaper in the old Victorian style hadn't been a bad idea, but once they'd finished papering the walls they hadn't been able to stop. Before they knew it the whole room was furnished in the Victorian style. "Looks good, doesn't it?" she said, smoothing the tiny bedspread.

"Here's another one," Wilfred said, as he set a large flat box on the other side of Jeanmarie's and Pearl's work. The box held a scene that made Jeanmarie think of one of her favorite books—*The Call of the Wild*. White clay mountains, trees, and creamy snow-packed trails surrounded the edges. A dogsled with miniature clay dogs painted to look like huskies pulled a sled with leather harnesses and toothpick runners. The lead dog, like the one in the story, was larger than the rest. Next to him stood a fur-bundled figure. A little way off a small canvas tent waited.

What at first escaped Jeanmarie's attention now held her spellbound. In among the trees and close to what she thought must be a frozen lake were traps! Paper clips twisted to look like traps! With the war on nobody had metal clips to spare. Where had Wilfred gotten them? Trails in the snow showed the winding line of animal traps, which evidently the sled had visited. As she looked closer she saw that piles of fur were tied to the sled. In front of the project lay a map of the trapping area carefully drawn in black ink, Wilfred's handiwork, no doubt.

"Like it?" Wilfred asked, pushing his glasses back on his nose.

Jeanmarie ran her fingers lightly over the fake snow. "It's good," she admitted, "really good." Wilfred liked art along with everything else that had to do with school, and he did well in it. She wondered how much of the work Sophie had done but asked instead, "Where on earth did you get the fur?"

"Right out of the earth," Wilfred said. "Used the fur from an old mitten one of the dogs dug up. Most of it was chewed, but it still had enough fur left to use."

Sophie came toward them, holding a booklet bound together with a leather shoelace. She laid it next to the art-work. "Finished it last night," she announced. "I've titled it 'A Day in the Life of a Hudson Bay Fur Trapper.'"

Wilfred smiled broadly at her. "Bet you did a terrific job too," he said.

Jeanmarie brushed past Sophie without a word as Mrs. Gillpin called for everyone in class to take their seats. Sophie might be good at writing reports, but she was still a thief, and one of these days Wilfred would find that out. Jeanmarie glanced at him and saw that once again his head was bent over a book the way the old Wilfred's usually was every spare minute he got. Curious, she thought about all those paper clips. Where had he gotten them? Long ago Mrs. Gillpin had told the class not to mind about clipping their papers since metal clips were so scarce. Even scrap paper was needed for the war effort. Jeanmarie looked at the notice hanging on the wall near the front of the classroom. In large letters it read, "To help meet the urgent wartime need for paper, every scrap must be salvaged for further use." It was the same for metal, including the foil wrappers on chewing gum. According to the newspaper the Germans even melted down iron bells from the church towers to use for the war. Her gaze wandered to Sophie's desk. Had she been the supplier? Were the clips from another one of her hoards of stolen stuff? She had to find out.

Saturday at the square dance, that's when she'd ask Wilfred. If there was one thing Wilfred hated, it was dancing. Whenever Dr. Werner announced that everyone must take a partner, Wilfred managed to slip away into the boys' room; the rest of the time he simply sat on one of the benches against the gym wall. After her appendix operation and Wilfred's broken arm, they'd sat together watching the others square off. She would sit at the back of the gym while the weekly brief cartoon and newsreel played, slip over to the wall benches just before the square dance began, find Wilfred, and see about those metal paper clips.

Her plan had gone well. Seated in the back row she watched as Dr. Werner signaled for quiet and the lights dimmed. The newsreel showed scenes from the war front. As pictures of Jews newly freed from a concentration camp in Germany filled the screen, Jeanmarie stared. She had never seen anything like the starved, bony bodies of men so thin they looked almost like walking skeletons and more like children than grown men. Some stared at the camera with large dark sunken eyes. The commentator was saying something about the liberation and hope, but Jeanmarie barely heard him. How could the Nazis have been so cruel?

Jeanmarie was glad for the short comedy that followed. By the time the lights came on and the square dancing began the comedy had done its work. She'd laughed until her stomach hurt. She looked around expectantly for Wilfred and felt a sudden jolt.

There, in the lineup for partners, Wilfred stood facing Sophie. Jeanmarie sat on the bench she'd chosen against the wall, her eyes smarting, her face warm as she watched Wilfred and his chosen partner, Sophie, whirling around. She wished she hadn't come. But staying home on Saturday nights wasn't really a choice since the only ones who could were either sick or on restrictions. She'd been neither. Anyway she didn't intend to sit on a bench all night. She'd only planned to stay there long enough to talk to Wilfred. Laughter from across the gym caught her attention. On a bench a handful of boys sat laughing and talking, one of them Ralph, the farmer's son. She knew he could see her.

"Hi, Nanny." Lizzie and May, each of them wearing red bows in their hair, stood in front of her. Both little motherless girls called her their Jeanmarie-Nanny. "Want to partner with us?" Lizzie offered.

Jeanmarie rubbed a smudge from Lizzie's chin. "No thanks. You two run along and have fun. I see Miss Bigler is about to start a square just for your size. Go on now." She watched the two bounce happily back to the corner of the gym reserved for the youngest children under the watchful eye of Miss Bigler, Dr. Werner's assistant. If only Jeanmarie could find a corner and dissolve into it, she would. No one came to claim her for a partner, and for the rest of the evening Jeanmarie sat by herself, wishing she were anywhere else.

At last Dr. Werner dismissed them. Jeanmarie hurried through the gym door, desperate to reach the welcome dark of the cool night air. Almost running she found herself alone on the girls' hill. Laughter and voices sounded from behind her as friends, in no hurry to leave, walked slowly. Jeanmarie increased her pace. She didn't want to talk to anyone tonight. Had she been looking where she was going instead of at the road she might have avoided crashing into the stranger ahead of her.

They bumped so hard, Jeanmarie's head butted straight into the man's back. "OOPH." The man spun around, his arm raised as if to strike. The startled look on his face as he saw

Jeanmarie turned to anger. Without a word he walked swiftly away toward the road through the orchard.

Jeanmarie stared after him. He was tall, dressed in a dark raincoat, and she had never seen him before! In a moment she heard the sound of a car pulling away. Who was he? What was he doing on the orphanage grounds this time of night? Jeanmarie turned back to Wheelock and stood thinking for a minute. She had run into the stranger right here, and his back was toward her. The man had been facing Wheelock! If he'd been coming out of the house, she would have run into him face on. Either he'd already been inside and come out, then stopped to look back, or he'd been about to go in. If he'd been about to go in, why had he left? She stared at the cottage but saw nothing unusual. He could be a friend of Mrs. Ripple's. But who'd visit this late? Maybe he'd lost his way and just stopped to ask directions and changed his mind.

Others were coming, and Jeanmarie hurried inside. Mrs. Ripple was going upstairs as she rushed in. "Oh, Mrs. Ripple, I just . . ." Jeanmarie began but got no further.

Holding to the rail, Mrs. Ripple turned slightly, enough so that Jeanmarie could see her face drained of all color. She raised one hand, said, "Not now, Jeanmarie, not now," and went slowly but steadily up the stairs without looking back. Jeanmarie heard her steps in the hall above and then the sound of a door shutting.

As if on cue, Pearl, who was on restrictions for forgetting to turn in homework three times in a row, appeared at the top of the staircase. Mrs. Gillpin's rule always held fast, though she looked as if it pained her each time she wrote out a restrictions note, especially one for Pearl. Whenever she was caught up in a good book, Pearl easily forgot all about homework. "Hi," she said. "Any luck with Wilfred?"

"No, but what's the matter with Mrs. Ripple? She looks terrible," Jeanmarie said in a low voice. "I was about to tell her I ran smack into a man standing outside the house a moment ago, but she never gave me the chance. Did Mrs. Ripple have company tonight?"

Pearl kept her voice low as Jeanmarie joined her. "No one's been here that I know of, and Mrs. Ripple was fine the last time I saw her just after all of you left. I've been in the dorm all night reading. What's this about a man?" She listened wide-eyed as Jeanmarie filled her in. When she finished, Pearl said quickly, "I didn't hear anything coming from downstairs except the radio somebody left on. All I heard were snatches of a program. One of the characters, a man, wanted money I think, but I've been wanting to read this book for ages so I didn't listen really. I guess I got involved in my book until a couple of minutes ago. Besides, who'd be visiting this time of night? And if he wasn't visiting what was he doing outside?" Her eyes grew wide again.

Jeanmarie stared at her. "When I came in, Mrs. Ripple was on her way upstairs. That means she was down here. Oh, Pearl, you know how you are once you get a book in your hands. Anybody could have come in and left before you noticed. I think that man was either about to come to the house or he'd already been and was just standing thinking about it, else why was he here in the first place? Something's going on," Jeanmarie said. "But what?"

EIGHT

A Sleepwalker

*T*he rest of the gang came trooping in, and in the general noise Jeanmarie slipped upstairs. Lifting the blackout curtain slightly she peered into the night but saw no one. The man hadn't come back, and by now the stranger and his car were well away from the orphanage. She undressed slowly, thinking of the events of the night. Across the room Winnie and the twins were getting ready for bed and reporting to Pearl what she had missed at the gym.

"Lights out, girls; good night," Mrs. Ripple said, entering the doorway and reaching for the light. She snapped the switch and then shut the door, plunging the dorm into total darkness. Mrs. Ripple had never closed the door before. Between the blackout curtains and the door shutting out the friendly night-light that spilled into the hallway from the small bathroom, Jeanmarie could almost feel the darkness like a thickness around her.

"What's going on?" Winnie asked.

Jeanmarie crept to the foot of her cot, felt for the heavy curtain and lifted it again. Pale moonlight entered, dispelling some of the night. "Plenty, and we need to talk," she said in a low voice as she tied a knot in the curtain to hold it back. She sat on the edge of her cot, waiting while Winnie and the others quickly joined her. In a whisper she filled them in on what had happened earlier.

Winnie, huddled between Pearl and the foot of Jeanmarie's cot asked, "Pearl, what if it wasn't the radio you heard? Suppose it was the man and Mrs. Ripple?" Winnie, who always tried to be fair, quickly added, "Of course you'd have recognized Mrs. Ripple's voice, so it probably was the radio. And the man could have just been lost and trying to decide whether or not to ask for directions when you scared him half out of his wits by crashing into him, Jem. Did either of you check to see if the radio really was playing?" Jeanmarie shook her head no.

"I didn't check either," Pearl whispered back. "I just figured it was on before I went upstairs to read. But, Winnie, I only heard snatches of voices, and I really couldn't make out the woman's words very well. They sounded kind of muffled. I don't know if what I heard was the radio or for real." Pearl shrugged her thin shoulders. "But we do know Jeanmarie ran into a man standing outside Wheelock, and he nearly hit her. Something made Mrs. Ripple go pale and shut herself in her room."

"Right," Jeanmarie agreed, "and look how she's shut the door on us tonight, which isn't at all like her." She sighed heavily, then yawned. "If some man *was* visiting Mrs. Ripple here and asking for money, who could it be? Who could Mrs.

Ripple owe money to?" She shivered and hugged her arms. "What about her stolen change purse?" she said. "Suppose it was stuffed full of money?" She sighed. "That doesn't make sense; it's too small to hold much. Nothing fits exactly." She stifled a yawn.

Winnie shook her head. "No; it doesn't make sense. I still think the poor man only wanted directions. Mrs. Ripple's been looking pale and worn out for days. Who wouldn't be, with all those poison pen letters and losing things." Winnie looked earnest. "Besides, you know how you get, Pearl, when you're reading."

"You mean I'd barely notice no matter what was going on? I guess so." Pearl was that kind of reader, and they all knew it. She had begun to shiver in the coolness. "But where are we then? If Win is right, maybe the stranger was just lost. How hard did you bump him, Jeanmarie?" She chuckled and went on, not waiting for an answer. "Let's suppose he has nothing to do with any of this. We know the letters have upset Mrs. Ripple. I've thought of another thing that might connect the phone calls and the thefts. Suppose something really valuable was in Mrs. Ripple's missing change purse, like a locket or a pin, a family heirloom someone in the family wants. If we find our thief's stash we might find the explanation."

The prickles that ran through Jeanmarie this time weren't just from the cold. Pearl made sense! Tired as she felt, the more she thought about it, the more it seemed likely that the stranger was innocent. It was wartime, and it had been dark when she'd run into him. No wonder she'd startled him so badly.

"Listen," Jeanmarie said, "so far all we really have to go on are the facts about Sophie." At the look on Tess's face she quickly added, "Or Leah maybe. But it's Sophie who's the only new person around here. The thefts and the letters to Mrs. Ripple started shortly after she came, and on top of that nobody knows much about her, or the straight story about her folks." She held up her hand. "Okay, I admit the facts about her folks could be explained if she's telling the truth." She paused before adding, "Then there's the taped-up box in her drawer." No one said anything as if they knew what she was thinking. "Think about it, okay? Whatever's in there could help us one way or the other." Pearl groaned, and Jeanmarie quickly added, "I don't mean tonight but soon." She didn't have a real plan yet.

For a long time Jeanmarie lay on her cot, listening to the soft breathing of the others who were already asleep. It wasn't Leah, it was Sophie who didn't add up. She didn't fit in, didn't try to except with Wilfred. The vision of Wilfred at the square dance with Sophie added to her misery. Sophie wasn't satisfied just to steal their stuff.

With the door shut Jeanmarie heard only the soft breathy sounds of the other girls and Winnie's light snoring. Had the door been open she might have heard the sound of muffled crying coming from the small dorm.

With her pillow over her head Sophie cried softly. Over and over the newsreel of the Jewish captives in Germany played in her head. "Mama, it is so terrible. Why, Mama, why?" After a long while the crying stopped, the pillow slipped to one side, and Sophie's eyes closed. Stillness fell upon Wheelock and its occupants.

Jeanmarie knew she'd been asleep, but something had awakened her. She sat up. As her eyes adjusted to the dark she saw a figure standing by Winnie's bed. "Winnie," she whispered. There was no answer. Like a slow moving shadow the figure glided to the door and out into the hall. Jeanmarie's heart beat loudly as she slipped out of bed. Winnie, snoring lightly, was still in her cot, and so were all the others. The thief, it must be her! She had to find out.

In the tiny gleam of light spilling into the hallway from the bathroom night-light, Sophie, wearing a white nightgown, walked slowly toward the stairway. She was halfway down the hall and looking straight ahead. Jeanmarie held her breath. Maybe this time she'd catch her in the act.

Instead of going down the stairs Sophie turned where the hall made an L shape that led to Mrs. Ripple's room. Jeanmarie followed quietly. Sophie was going straight into the housemother's room! Jeanmarie gasped and stood where she was. Should she follow her? What if Mrs. Ripple woke up? What if she didn't and Sophie took something? This time she wouldn't get away with it even if it meant telling Mrs. Ripple everything in the middle of the night!

Almost as suddenly as she'd gone into the room Sophie came out and headed straight toward Jeanmarie. Jeanmarie stared at her, but Sophie didn't seem to see her at all. As the girl drew closer Jeanmarie instinctively flattened herself against the wall to let her pass. Sophie walked like someone in a dream. Her eyes were open, but they might as well have been closed as she glided past Jeanmarie. A few steps away Mrs. Ripple, her unbound hair hanging down around her waist and a robe thrown across her shoulders, appeared in her doorway. She put a finger to her lips, motioning Jeanmarie to be silent. Could Sophie be sleepwalking? If she had stolen something it wasn't visible to Jeanmarie.

Quickly Mrs. Ripple moved to stand between Sophie and the stairs. For a moment Sophie paused as if sensing something, turned away from the stairs, and glided toward the small dorm. Mrs. Ripple walked quietly behind her, and Jeanmarie followed. From the doorway they watched as Sophie made her way to her bed and climbed in. They waited for a few minutes, but Sophie didn't stir.

Mrs. Ripple put an arm around Jeanmarie's shoulder and led her back into the hallway. "I fear our poor Sophie is a sleepwalker," she whispered. "I must report this to the school nurse. Something is troubling the poor child. Whatever it is she hasn't shared it. I suppose losing her parents and coming to the orphanage is all part of it. Some people hold their feelings inside, and whatever is bothering them comes out in another form."

"Like sleepwalking?" Jeanmarie whispered.

"Yes, it just might be that." Mrs. Ripple stopped at the door to the large dorm. "Do you think you can go back to sleep now? I'll listen for her a while, and I'll put a chair in front of the stairs just in case. We don't want her falling down the steps."

"Right," Jeanmarie said. For a moment she'd felt the warmth of Mrs. Ripple's arm and almost forgotten everything else. It had reminded her of her mother long ago. She turned and walked slowly back to her cot past the others, who were sleeping soundly. Back in bed she huddled under the blanket. Sleepwalking! How could someone steal things in their sleep? Was that when she did it? Did Sophie know what she was doing? No one could be that good an actor. She really had been asleep, hadn't she?

In the morning a high-backed armchair stood against the wall in the small alcove between the attic stairs and the stairway to the first floor. Jeanmarie recognized it as one from Mrs. Ripple's sewing room. At least she knew she hadn't been dreaming about last night.

The girls stood waiting in the dining room for Mrs. Ripple to say grace. Jeanmarie stole a look at Sophie, whose face was turned away. Like the rest of them Sophie wore a Sunday outfit—a green blouse with a print skirt. The blouse certainly showed up Sophie's red hair. Sophie turned as Mrs. Ripple began grace, and their eyes met for an instant before Jeanmarie closed hers. There had been no hint of recognition—nothing unusual.

With a questioning look Pearl handed Jeanmarie a plate of dark toast. "Did she give any sign about last night?" she asked in a low voice.

Jeanmarie shook her head. She'd told the others about Sophie's sleepwalking. "The worst of it is," she whispered back, "though I don't think she was pretending, we can't be really sure." She sighed as she picked up the crisp bread with its blackened crusts. They couldn't watch Sophie day and night. Jeanmarie bit into her toast. She didn't mind a little burnt toast. It was the burnt oatmeal waiting in front of her that she couldn't stomach.

"There has to be some kind of record here," Pearl whispered. "Only I'm losing count. Next to burnt soup I detest burnt oatmeal."

At the table across the room someone else was counting, not food items but hours. Sophie glanced at the wall clock. In exactly five hours the visitors' bus would arrive. If all went as planned she would have her chance.

The morning passed swiftly. Lunch had come and gone, and Wheelock was nearly deserted. Sophie waited until she was sure the others were gone, most of them to meet the bus. Leah had left to visit friends in other cottages. Mrs. Ripple was up in her rooms. It was the perfect time.

Quietly, Sophie crept up the stairs and down the hallway to the small dorm. She might not have much time before someone came. In the corner where the young ones shared a dresser with Leah and herself she carefully pulled out the middle drawer. Lizzie's. Feeling beneath the neatly piled garments her fingers closed on something. She drew it out and looked at it. The sound of a door opening startled her, and she dropped the object into her pocket, shut the drawer, and moved away from the dresser. She would have to wait and think. She needed a plan.

Down at the main gate to the orphanage grounds Jeanmarie held Lizzie's hand while they watched the few visitors climb from the bus. Jeanmarie had half hoped her father wouldn't come. Relief that he hadn't flooded her. When the empty bus pulled away she felt the small hand tug at hers. "Let's go, Nanny. Granny couldn't come again. Maybe her feet swelled up like the last time." The little girl's face looked woeful.

Jeanmarie knelt down and brushed away the tears that were spilling down Lizzie's face. "Now, you know your granny loves you, Lizzie. I'm sure she would have come if she could. I just bet she'll be here when the weather turns warm. Why don't you make her a nice spring picture and send it to her so she'll feel better?"

Lizzie sniffed, hugged Jeanmarie around the neck, and ran off, calling for her friend May. With a heavy feeling Jeanmarie watched the little girl go. Only once had her grandmother visited, and that was two years ago.

"Coming?" Pearl called from the gate. Beside her the twins waited, looking alike in spite of the pink dress of the one and the yellow dress of the other. Jeanmarie waved. Her conscience pricked her. Lizzie wanted her granny to visit so much, and she, Jeanmarie, was glad her father didn't come.

He was her father, and she supposed she should be just a little sorry but not today.

"Coming," she called to the others. They needed to plan their next move. Sophie's sleepwalking had only made things more difficult.

NINE

The Clue

R ed," Jeanmarie whispered to herself. She stared at the single hair lying in the palm of her hand. Behind her Pearl let out her breath, and Jeanmarie turned, holding her palm up. "This is it," she said. "The evidence we needed." Sophie was their thief; no doubt about it. The red hair had been caught on the inside of Jeanmarie's dresser drawer in the loose screw that held the drawer pull. She'd noticed it because it lay close to where her last bobby pin had been. The pin was nowhere in the drawer. Triumphantly, Jeanmarie pinched the hair between her thumb and forefinger, holding it up for Winnie and the twins to see. "There's no way this could have gotten into my drawer unless the thief unknowingly left it there. Now all we have to do is confront her."

"Wait a minute," Pearl said. "Suppose she really doesn't know what she's doing? I mean, if she's asleep when she takes things, then what?"

Jeanmarie looked at the red hair in her hand. "Maybe. But she didn't have anything in her hands when I saw her sleepwalking. How could she do it? And where is all the stuff? Besides, she couldn't possibly write poison pen letters in her sleep."

"I forgot about the letters," Pearl said. "There's no way we can explain them."

"Aren't we forgetting something else?" Tess asked. "We still don't know what's in the taped box, and I think we ought to find out first before we do anything else."

"I agree," Maria added. "Sophie could say we're just trying to blame her, and that anyone could have found a red hair in the bathroom, or even taken one from her hairbrush and left it in the drawer."

Jeanmarie frowned. "But you're all my witnesses. You saw me take it from the drawer."

Quietly Tess remarked, "But, remember, we didn't see who put it in there."

"You mean you're still not convinced Sophie is the thief? Don't tell me you think Leah is the thief. The swelling in her hands has gone down, but she still has poison ivy."

"Maybe," Tess said, "but nothing's been taken all the time Leah's hands were so swollen. You can't deny it looks suspicious."

Pearl nodded. "Anyway, accusing Sophie doesn't mean she's going to admit anything. We have a single red hair. It wouldn't stand up in a courtroom."

For the first time, Jeanmarie felt defeated. "Does anybody besides me think Sophie's guilty?" No one answered.

Winnie leaned over to pat her arm. "Pearl's right. Even if she is our thief we still need more proof. And we don't know yet what's in the box." A hard cough interrupted her. As it left she pressed a hand to her chest.

Concern flooded Jeanmarie. "Win, are you okay?" she asked.

"It's spring, you know," Winnie's voice rasped. "I didn't expect it to come so suddenly, but here it is." Every spring, Winnie suffered spells of coughing, wheezing, and sometimes fever. Winter and fall brought her low too, but in spring the attacks seemed even worse. Maria motioned Winnie to sit beside her on the bed. "Thanks," Winnie said, pulling a worn handkerchief from her pocket.

Jeanmarie carefully replaced the hair in the drawer where she had found it. "So you're all telling me that we need to catch her in the act? If it is Sophie." The red hair left no doubt in her mind who it was.

"Well, there's the box," Tess insisted. "We could open it, then tape it back just like it was before. That way we'd still have time to plan the next step."

"Tape it?" Pearl echoed. She looked quickly at Jeanmarie, then at the others. "Who has any tape? We used every speck we could find on our art project. I know Leah gave us all she had left."

Maria looked glum as she shook her head. "None here."

"Maybe if we're careful, we can use the same tape to put it back together," Jeanmarie said hopefully. "Or what about Mrs. Gillpin? She might have some to spare."

"I need to mend my spelling book," Winnie offered. "I could ask for the tape to do it at home."

"That's it," Tess cried. "All we have to do is whisk the box away just long enough to open it. The whole thing shouldn't take more than ten minutes." Her dark eyes were eager.

Jeanmarie nodded. "Right, but which ten minutes? We'll have to wait until Sophie is out, and no one else is in the dorm. I guess that's it; we watch and wait." Disappointment gripped her. "You get the tape, Win. We'll find a time," she said. Thankfully they wouldn't have to wait a whole weekend. Winnie could ask Mrs. Gillpin this morning.

In class Jeanmarie let her thoughts wander until she heard the word *war*. She'd almost forgotten the war! Mrs. Gillpin continued reading the morning news to the class. In some villages the Germans were fighting from house to house, and it seemed to Jeanmarie that they would never give up. Anxiously she searched Mrs. Gillpin's face. She knew Mr. Gillpin was still somewhere overseas. He'd been wounded once already. The teacher's face looked calm.

Mrs. Gillpin laid the paper on her desk and smiled. "Today, class, we have a special treat. Dr. Werner has given permission for our first three winners in the art projects to spend the rest of the morning visiting the lower grades to show and explain their work," she said. "Now for the grand announcements. I was so pleased with all your efforts, class, and hard-pressed to choose, but with Miss Bigler's help we've made our decisions. Our first-place winners are Sophie and Wilfred for their fine work on the Hudson Bay fur trappers." A roar of applause followed. Jeanmarie bit her lip.

"Our second-place winner is Martin for his wonderful puppet theater." Surrounded by cheers and claps, Martin, a small boy with a thatch of straw-colored hair, grinned.

"Last, but by no means least, we have Pearl and Jeanmarie for their charming Victorian room. Now let's all give ourselves a good hand for a truly successful display of art." The class clapped, and Jeanmarie smiled and clapped too, but her heart wasn't in it. They would have to spend the next two hours walking around together with Sophie and Wilfred.

The one bright spot in the day came when Winnie triumphantly held up the roll of tape she had borrowed. Jeanmarie glanced across the room at Sophie, whose head was bent above her reading book. What would they find in the taped box? As Sophie sighed and shifted in her seat, Jeanmarie thought of something she didn't want to think about—Sophie's sleepwalking. Ever since the other night a chair had been placed at the top of the stairway to block it just in case Sophie walked in her sleep again. Could guilt make a person sleepwalk? Jeanmarie wondered. Worse, was it possible she did steal in her sleep? And the red hair in her drawer—had Sophie been asleep or awake then?

The book in Jeanmarie's hand might as well have been written in Chinese. She couldn't concentrate at all. Something about the letters Mrs. Ripple kept getting nagged her. Like a light going on it struck her! All of them were mailed off grounds. How could Sophie manage that without leaving the orphanage grounds? Jeanmarie knew there wasn't a mailbox close to the orphanage. Sophie didn't go for walks off grounds like the rest of them. She couldn't have mailed those letters. Who did?

From her desk nearby Winnie coughed long and hard. Her face went from red to a terrible white that frightened Jeanmarie. Jeanmarie was about to pass her own clean handkerchief to Winnie when Mrs. Gillpin headed their way. She too had heard Winnie's cough. "Winifred, you don't sound at all well to me," Mrs. Gillpin said. "I'm sending you straight to Miss Bigler. I believe the school nurse is due in this afternoon."

The nurse had sent Winnie home with a note. By the time Jeanmarie arrived at Wheelock Winnie's voice was a mere squeak. A pile of tissues and a glass with a thermometer in it sat next to the bed. "Can't talk," Winnie managed. "Forgot the tape; sorry."

Jeanmarie tucked the blanket up around Winnie's shoulders. "Never mind the tape. Just get better. We can wait," she said. Winnie smiled, then closed her eyes. Jeanmarie left quietly. The waiting would be hard. More than ever she had to know what was in that taped box.

In the hallway Mrs. Ripple stood talking into the phone. "Yes, bed rest for the next few days. I'll do that, and I will call you if her temperature goes too high. Honey with thyme mixed in ought to help with that cough. . . . Right." Jeanmarie slipped past Mrs. Ripple and headed downstairs. Poor Winnie.

By Friday, thanks to Winnie, who was still in bed, not a single thing had disappeared from the dorm, though Tess was certain someone had taken her last small sliver of pink soap. She'd left it on the tub and by the time she went back for it, the soap was gone.

"It really was such a tiny piece," Maria said, "that I can't imagine why anyone would want to steal it."

Tess's eyes widened. "Small or not, it still smelled like lavender. I could have made it last, you know."

Winnie, her voice hoarse, added, "Tess's soap disappeared from the washroom during the day, right? So we can be pretty sure our thief works in the daytime." Carefully, she moved a checker on the red-and-black board in front of her and jumped Maria's king. "One good thing's come out of my being in bed all week—nobody has dared come in here to take anything."

Maria edged her remaining checker into a corner. "Guess I'm through," she said.

"That's brilliant, Win, and I don't mean jumping Maria's king," Jeanmarie said. Now she was certain Sophie didn't steal in her sleep. All the evidence pointed to thefts during the day, and Sophie had plenty of opportunities while the rest of them were at work. That is until this week when Winnie had been here to prevent her.

From the doorway Pearl called, "Hurry up, the rest of you, or you'll be late for supper!"

As Jeanmarie caught up with her at the top of the stairs, Pearl made a sad face. "Don't forget, I have a return visit to the dentist tomorrow. Mrs. Ripple just told me Dr. Werner will pick me up after lunch. I guess you'll have to work alone again at the Shapiros'. The good news is you get to eat all the goodies; the bad news is you have to do all the work."

If only Jeanmarie had known how bad the news really was.

TEN

Sophie and the Menorah

Mrs. Ripple's tone of voice made it clear she had already decided that Sophie should take Pearl's place working for the Shapiros this Saturday. "So you will show her the way and tell her what is expected," she said to Jeanmarie. "I think it will do Sophie good to get off grounds. You might get to know her a little better this way too," she added.

Jeanmarie swallowed hard. The last thing in the world she wanted was to bring Sophie to the Shapiros'. "Yes, ma'am."

Mrs. Ripple nodded and hurried off to the kitchen with an anxious look on her face. Jeanmarie sniffed the air but couldn't detect the smell of anything burning. Her thoughts returned to the hours ahead of her with Sophie.

By the time they reached the Shapiros' cottage, Sophie hadn't spoken more than three words. Jeanmarie had tried making conversation, explained the work they'd have to do, even pointed out some wildflowers near the path, but she'd finally given up. They'd walked in complete silence for the last stretch.

Mrs. Shapiro met them at the door. As Jeanmarie explained about Sophie, Mrs. Shapiro gently reached out to touch Sophie's red hair. "Such beautiful hair," she said. "Red as wine kissed by the sun, Aunt Miriam would say, may she rest in peace." Sophie seemed to flinch at her touch. A look of surprise flitted across Mrs. Shapiro's face and she dropped her hand quickly. Then she smiled warmly and ushered them in, all the while chatting about the warm spring day. "So now, help yourselves to the goodies," she urged.

When Mrs. Shapiro disappeared down the hall toward the porch Jeanmarie took a roll and bit into it. "Mmm, delicious," she said, holding out the plate to Sophie.

Sophie's face had gone white. She stared at the dainty little rolls and shook her head.

"You okay?" Jeanmarie asked.

"Fine," Sophie replied. She turned toward the sink, her back to Jeanmarie. "I'll wash if it's okay with you," she said. Her voice sounded hoarse.

"Fine," Jeanmarie retorted. If Sophie didn't want to be friendly, then she wouldn't bother either. Neither of them spoke until the dishes were done.

Reaching for the mop, Jeanmarie saw the tablecloth move slightly where it hung low over the edge almost to the floor. She knew it had to be David under there. She would just wait until he decided to come out. What she didn't expect was Sophie's reaction when the small boy suddenly emerged.

The cup in Sophie's hand went flying, struck the edge of the table, and broke. Sophie's eyes were wide, her face white with terror. David screamed, stood frozen for a second, then ran. The door to the porch slammed.

Mrs. Shapiro came hurrying into the kitchen. "Girls, is anyone hurt?" she cried.

"No, I don't think so," Jeanmarie said, glancing at Sophie, who looked as though she might faint. "David was hiding under the table, and Sophie didn't know," she said. "I guess when the cup accidentally shattered it frightened David. Is he alright?"

Mrs. Shapiro's friend, an older woman with graying hair bound in a tight bun, had come to the doorway. "Oy vey, such a boy. Always hiding. And now look, your beautiful china in pieces. My David, he is not hurt, but your cup, oy vey."

"No, no, Ada, the cup is nothing; it was here when we bought the cottage." Using the edge of a napkin Mrs. Shapiro bent to sweep the broken bits into a pile. "You mustn't mind, girls; little boys will be boys. No one is hurt; for that we can be thankful."

As the two women left, Jeanmarie heard the visitor say, "A little boy he should be, but this one—he is like a little old man, scared of his own shadow, I tell you."

Sophie shook her head like someone waking up. "I didn't mean it," she said, staring at the remains of the cup lying in the dustbin.

Jeanmarie felt a faint flash of guilt. She hadn't warned Sophie that David was under the table. "Accidents happen," she said as cheerily as she could manage. After that the afternoon went by quickly. David did not reappear, and Jeanmarie supposed he had gone out to play.

Sophie seemed to have recovered from her fright and worked hard, speaking only to ask what she should do next. Once when Jeanmarie came back to the kitchen for another cloth, Sophie was wiping the brass candlestick holder called a menorah. It looked like a tree with four branches on each side for each of the eight candles and a center holder for a ninth candle. From the doorway Jeanmarie watched as Sophie traced each branch with her finger. When Sophie gently set it back on the shelf Jeanmarie saw her touch her lips and then the menorah with the slightest kiss, sort of the way Jeanmarie had seen one of the orphan boys do to the Saint Joseph medal around his neck just before a ball game. Jeanmarie shook her head. Didn't Sophie know any better? Why would she kiss a Jewish candlestick? Unless. . . .

A terrible thought brought goosebumps to the back of Jeanmarie's neck. Sophie wouldn't dream of stealing something from the Shapiros, would she? The menorah was too big, but there were other things, smaller items that could slip easily into a pocket. If Sophie liked the menorah so much there was no telling what else she might take a fancy to. As Sophie turned, her eyes met Jeanmarie's. Her face flushed.

Jeanmarie lowered her gaze to the rag in her hand. "I'll help you dust," she said. "We can work together and finish one room at a time." Jeanmarie didn't dare leave her alone. For the remainder of their time she would have to watch her every minute.

It had taken longer, but at last they were done. Mrs. Shapiro came to pay them. "Such a beautiful job, who could believe it," she said. "I have here in my pocket your pay, and oh my, what is this?" From her pocket she pulled out a six-pointed star. Jeanmarie had seen it before. "David's star," Mrs. Shapiro said. "He left it on the porch, and I forgot to give it to him. Such a boy," she added and smiled, holding the star in her palm.

From the corner of her eye Jeanmarie saw Sophie staring at the star as though she had never seen one before. Thankfully, Mrs. Shapiro put it back into her pocket and brought out two crisp dollar bills. At least Sophie couldn't get her hands on that star. Jeanmarie took the money and handed one bill to Sophie, while Mrs. Shapiro placed some rolls in a paper bag for Pearl.

The door had barely closed behind them when Sophie took off in a steady jog without so much as a word of explanation. Jeanmarie didn't go after her. She knows I saw her with the menorah and doesn't want to talk, Jeanmarie thought. But it was only a matter of time now before Sophie would have to admit to the thefts; meanwhile she could find her own way back to Wheelock. Jeanmarie walked slowly down the path and onto the road. The evidence might not be the hard kind yet, but it was piling up.

A tall, familiar frame stepped from the woods just ahead of her—Ralph, the last person she wanted to see. Jeanmarie quickened her steps to pass him by. Ralph quickened his, then slowed his long legs to keep pace with her. "Go away," Jeanmarie said. "I'm in a hurry."

"Please," Ralph begged. "I can explain about last week. I mean, I can't tell you or anybody why my pa is so pigheaded about some things. It's just his way." Ralph kept at her side no matter how quickly Jeanmarie walked. "Pa's scair't I'll quit school and never amount to much. He's set on me being a farmer with my own farm one day. But it's not what I want. I'm aiming to be a veterinarian like my uncle Joe." Ralph was quiet for a minute. "Pa don't mean any harm. It wasn't you he was mad at. It was me. He's a prideful man, like his daddy before him. I'm not like him. I hate it when he acts the way he did the other day. Jeanmarie, you listening to me? Could you just slow down and listen a minute?"

Jeanmarie kept her eyes straight ahead. "How do you know your pa won't come roaring down this road any minute?"

"He won't," Ralph said. "He can't leave the freezer house until they're done, at least another hour from now," Ralph's voice pleaded. "Maybe you don't want to hear it, but I'm gonna say it: I don't care if you're an orphan. It's not your fault." Ralph looked miserable as Jeanmarie glared at him. "Nobody should have to be one. I guess it's sort of like having a broken wing only it can't get mended," he said. Jeanmarie poked him hard with her elbow.

"Don't you get it?" Ralph shouted. "I'm going to be a veterinarian. I'll take care of you." Ralph's face was beet red, and he had stopped walking.

Jeanmarie stood still. "I'm not an orphan it just so happens, but if I was, I'd still be me; orphan or not, I'd still be me. I don't need your help. You just better go on before your pa sees you." She could feel her own face hot and angry. Looking straight in front of her she walked quickly toward the orphanage. She didn't look back. Her own words rang inside her, "I'd still be me; orphan or not, I'd still be me."

There was no sound behind her. Ralph must be standing back there, or maybe he'd gone into the woods so she wouldn't see him pass. She kept walking and listening but heard nothing. She didn't want his company anyway, not now. She had enough to think about with Sophie and the menorah. A bird chirped loudly from a nearby tree. A robin, she thought.

ELEVEN

Sam Helps Out

"I t's about time you showed up," Wilfred said, stepping in front of Jeanmarie just as she reached the corner of the school building. "Knew you'd have to pass this way but thought you'd be done with work half an hour ago." He held out a small box with holes in the top and a note attached to it. "Here."

Puzzled, Jeanmarie took the box. "What's this for?" she asked. Something moved inside, nearly making her drop the package. "What's in it?" she demanded. "If it's alive I don't want it, and anyway, why are you giving it to me?"

"Ralph sent it. He said you'd know what to do." Wilfred had already begun walking away. He headed toward the boys' hill. "Got to go; I'm late."

Jeanmarie knew what was in the box as she set it down on the road. "I don't want it!" she called to Wilfred. "You can just take it back to Ralph and tell him to keep it himself." Frustrated she watched as Wilfred waved once and quickened his pace away from her. "Why me?" she said aloud, bending to retrieve the box. Carefully she held it close. The annoyed chirping from inside confirmed her guess. It had to be the baby sparrow. While she walked with the box in one arm, she read the note.

It was from Ralph. "I know you will take care of him for me. I've listed things he likes to eat and what to do to keep the box clean. In a few weeks, maybe sooner, the wing should be better, and you can take the splints off. If it looks okay, then you can let him start exercising it. One of these days he'll fly away, like me. I'm going to do what I should've done in the first place. One day when I'm a veterinarian, maybe you'll be the one sending something with a broken wing instead of me sending you the sparrow. Take care of him. Ralph."

Jeanmarie pushed the note deep into her pocket. Ralph had run away. The rest of the way to Wheelock she scarcely saw the road or anything else. It wasn't her fault he'd gone. But if she hadn't been so mean, maybe if she'd listened to him, she could have helped him. Had he gone to his uncle Joe's? Where else would he go? Unless he went to the city to find a job. The city could be a mean place for kids like Ralph with no one to look out for them. What would his father do when he found out? Jeanmarie didn't dare think about it. The box in her hands tilted, sending off flutters and chirpings inside. Where in the world would she keep the baby bird? Even if the weather felt more and more like spring, she couldn't keep it outside. Not with the stray cats she'd seen visiting the grounds.

The cellar, divided as it was into furnace room, storage room, and coatroom, held the only possibility for hiding the baby bird, at least for now. Beyond the coal bins, out of sight behind the giant old furnace, was a small window with a wide stone ledge. It would have to do. Jeanmarie opened the box and picked up the baby sparrow. Its splinted wing stuck out awkwardly as she cradled the bird in her hands. "I'll be back," she promised, returning it to its box on the ledge.

The others were already piling into the dining room for supper as she hurried in. They'd no sooner sat down when Pearl whispered, "Have we got news for you."

"Me too," Jeanmarie whispered back, "but you go first."

The twins and Winnie leaned in close to listen as Pearl explained. "Tess brought another letter today for Mrs. Ripple, and this time on the return address side someone stamped 'Slate Hotel.'" She paused, and Tess nodded in agreement.

"That's it? Just Slate Hotel?" Jeanmarie tried to keep her voice low. "What about the address?"

"There wasn't any," Pearl insisted. "Look, it's a start. All we have to do is find out where the hotel is and who sent the letter. Right?"

"It's not much to go on, but I guess it's better than nothing," Jeanmarie said. Her mind was still on the baby sparrow.

"Okay, what is it you've got for us? You said you had news," Pearl demanded.

"You aren't going to believe this," Jeanmarie began. She glanced around to make sure no one at the nearby tables looked too interested. "We've got a visitor, a permanent one, or until it gets well anyway," she said. The others had stopped eating. Winnie's eyes were wide. In a whisper voice Jeanmarie told them about Ralph and the baby sparrow. "We've got a new orphan. I'll show you later," she promised.

"We'll need plenty of these," Winnie said in a take-charge tone of voice, gathering crumbs from the table into her napkin. With a startled look on her face she added, "You don't suppose we have to crush worms too?"

Happily the outside of the ground level cellar window was shielded with a low curved metal piece. The metal shield prevented anyone from accidentally stepping into the low depression in front of the window. It also made an excellent cover for anything left on the ledge inside.

Pretending to be absorbed by the book in her hand, Tess leaned against the wall in the hallway close to the door that led downstairs to the cellar. On the other side of the door at the top of the stairs Winnie stood listening for any signal from her. By the time Jeanmarie and the others had finished, the new nest looked quite comfortable. The larger box with its higher walls wouldn't need a top while the baby sparrow's wing was still healing. It could barely hop from the cozy nest to reach its feed box.

Jeanmarie had followed Ralph's list of what to do for the bird. Remembering the caged canary she'd once seen, she'd added a few ideas of her own. The new box was weighted to the ledge by a brick so that it couldn't fall. The nest from Ralph now had soft feathers from Winnie's pillow to line it. On the cellar side, a coarse burlap rag was draped casually in front of the box and hid it from view. Jeanmarie doubted anyone ever came past the furnace into this corner, or if they did, they probably wouldn't notice the old window high on the wall.

Back in the dorm Jeanmarie put her crumpled note from Ralph into the keepsake box she kept under her bed. Inside it a small carved bird gleamed from its own little nest of tissue. She closed the box and sighed.

"Don't worry," Pearl urged. "We'll all help with the sparrow. Winnie's already planning how to keep him stuffed." Across the room Winnie chuckled.

"It's not that," Jeanmarie said, seating herself on the floor and leaning the back of her head against the bed. Sadness filled her as she thought of Ralph somewhere in the night with no place to call his own. She swallowed hard.

Pearl seated herself near. "Time for a meeting, right?" she said. "You've probably already started thinking how we're going to find out about that hotel."

Jeanmarie hadn't given the hotel a thought, but as the others joined them a plan started to form. "Sam, the bus driver," she said. "His room at the farmhouse is full of pictures of hotels where he and his fishing buddies go." She'd dusted it enough times to know. "He might have heard of the place." He had a sharp tongue as well as a bad limp that had kept him out of the war, but she liked the gruff old bachelor. Monday couldn't come soon enough. Meanwhile down in the cellar one small baby sparrow needed watching.

Feeding the sparrow, worrying about him, and keeping the whole thing secret had taken up the weekend. Monday afternoon found Jeanmarie on her way to the farmhouse, rehearsing what she would say to Sam when she got there. The last person she wanted to see was the farmer's wife, Ralph's mother, but the small thin woman was headed right in her direction.

When the woman drew close enough her eyes met Jeanmarie's. The woman's gaunt face looked weary. Her eyes were red, and it was obvious she had been crying hard. Jeanmarie's stomach sank, but the woman said nothing as she hurried past. No one at Wheelock had heard anything about Ralph's whereabouts. Rumors from the boys who worked with the farmer said Ralph had just disappeared. A sudden shame filled Jeanmarie. Had Ralph left his mother a note? Should she show her the one he'd sent her with the sparrow? Angry as she'd felt toward Ralph's father, she could only feel an awful sorrow for his mother.

At the farmhouse, while Mrs. Koppel stayed in the kitchen, Jeanmarie followed Sam into the long hallway as he left the dining room. "Sam, can I see you for a minute?" she asked.

"What do you mean, see me? I'm standing here big as life, and you've got your two eyes, so what is it you want?" he answered gruffly, holding his pipe in one hand.

Jeanmarie grinned. That was Sam. "It's kind of a project," she said. "I need to find out about some things. I know you travel a lot, especially when you're on those fishing trips. Did you ever hear of the Slate Hotel? I'm wondering where it is, maybe the address," she said hopefully.

"Project, is it? Gimme a day to think about it. Now scram." The bus driver limped off, lighting his pipe as he went. Jeanmarie heard him chuckle.

The next morning as Jeanmarie, with her arms full of fresh towels, knocked on Sam's door, it swung open as if he had been waiting for her. "Got it," he said. "The Slate Hotel's in Pearl River not so far away. And it's not such a great hotel either, in case you're thinking of staying there." He laughed. "I sure wouldn't," he added.

"Why not?" Jeanmarie asked boldly.

"Cheap, run-down place, mostly for down-on-their-luck salesmen and that kind. You're not running away now, are you?" He looked questioningly at her over his pipe.

"Not on your life," Jeanmarie replied. "Guess I'm planning on riding the high school bus with you, Sam. It's likely I'll be here until I'm eighteen. I don't mind really."

Sam held his pipe in his hand for a moment, then replaced it between his teeth. "So alright then, go on, scram, and leave me some peace, kid." He handed her a small piece of paper with the words Pearl River written on it, took the towels, and waved her off.

Pearl's idea was brilliant. All they'd have to do was find the hotel phone number and a phone. Winnie or the twins would have to make the call. "You know the two of us will be off grounds at work, and on Sunday everything's closed. One of you can make the call off grounds while we're at the Shapiros'," she begged. But all three shook their heads adamantly.

"In that case we'll just have to do it ourselves," Jeanmarie said. "Before Saturday."

"Impossible," Pearl exclaimed. "Nobody gets off-ground passes on a weekday, and besides there's school and work. You can't be thinking up another scheme to go after dark or something. We could get into big trouble going against the rules. Besides, nothing's open then, and it would be plain crazy."

Jeanmarie tossed one of her braids behind her shoulder. Someone had to make the call, and the quicker the better. It meant breaking a rule, but only this once and just long enough to make the call. "I think we can do it tomorrow at lunchtime," she stated. The look of dawning wonder on the faces around her made her go on quickly. "We skip lunch and go right from class out the door before anyone notices. You know Mrs. Gillpin never goes into the lunchroom. So who's going to guess that we aren't on our way to some assignment or other? When we come to the trees off the road near Wheelock we turn in and we're out of sight. If we stick to the orchard we can be on the main road into town and reach the filling station in no time."

Barely pausing for breath she went on. "The store has a pay phone, and old Mr. Jones is deaf as a post. One of us keeps him busy while the other one makes the call. Then presto—we're on our way back before anybody's noticed we aren't there. When the bell rings we slip in along with the rest." It sounded so possible that she almost convinced herself it had to be a good plan, except for one small thing: Mrs. Gillpin expected them to be in the lunchroom. Jeanmarie swallowed hard. Mrs. Gillpin trusted her. This one time for Mrs. Ripple's sake it had to be okay. She was sure they could do it.

"One hour is all we have for lunch and recess," Pearl groaned. "What if we don't make it?"

But they had made it quietly out of school carrying their lunch bags and all the way to the small store. Jeanmarie dialed the hotel's number and waited. The clerk was busy with a customer, and Jeanmarie held the phone so Pearl could listen with her. "Hello, yes," she said into the receiver. "I'm calling for a client—Mrs. Ripple. The bill you sent her isn't clear. Would you please look it up, sir?"

A young-sounding man on the other end of the phone hesitated, then said gruffly, "What bill? Didn't send any bill. Ripple, you said? Wait a minute; you talking about Jay Ripple? He owes all right, big time. Say, who is this?"

At her end of the phone Jeanmarie carefully replaced the phone into its cradle. A Mr. Ripple? Mrs. Ripple's husband? Puzzled, Jeanmarie looked at Pearl. "All this time we thought she was a widow."

Between bites of lunch they ran to make it back to the orphanage on time. Jeanmarie puzzled over the news. "Mrs. Ripple let everyone think she's a widow. The way the hotel clerk said her husband owed big time, sounded like she has good reason not to want him around." A stone skittered under her shoe. She didn't slow up. Thankfully, the orchard was all downhill from here.

Pearl swerved to miss a bush. "All those letters from him; no wonder she can't keep her mind on cooking. Poor Mrs. Ripple. He must have been awful for her to leave him. Do you think they're divorced?"

The idea hadn't occurred to Jeanmarie. "If she is, maybe that's why she never mentioned him and let us think he was dead. She couldn't bear the shame," she said, waving the large oatmeal cookie in her hand. Divorce was something you didn't talk about. They reached the orphanage grounds just as Dr. Werner's car pulled up in front of them.

A deep frown creased his forehead as he stepped from the car. His voice sounded like low thunder to Jeanmarie. "Can you explain why you are not both at lunch with your class? And why I should discover you off grounds obviously hurrying back from who knows where?" he demanded. Jeanmarie stared at him speechless.

Pearl cleared her throat. "Sir," she began, "I, we, went to the store up the road," she said lamely. She too seemed at a loss for words.

Dr. Werner glared, his black eyes pools of indignation. "I suppose you have a good reason for such an undertaking?" Without waiting for an answer he pointed to the cookie in Jeanmarie's hand. "I do not consider running off without permission to buy cookies a reason." Dr. Werner stood stiff and tall. "Half the world is starving because of the war while we have food enough for all of us. I believe the orphanage provides sound nutrition for you. Your behavior has been inexcusably reckless and selfish. You've not only acted wildly but with utter disregard for the rules of this orphanage." Jeanmarie felt her heart beating wildly.

"Yes, sir," Pearl whispered, looking at the ground.

"Look at me," Dr. Werner commanded. Both girls obeyed at once. "You will consider yourselves grounded for the next month at which time I will review your case. I shall expect an apology and an essay on the importance of rules and of keeping them by tomorrow morning on my desk. You will report to Miss Bigler's office at the beginning of each lunch hour where you will eat your lunch and spend the remainder of the hour assisting Miss Bigler as she wishes until further notice. I shall myself speak to Mrs. Gillpin as soon as I drive you back to school."

Ushering Jeanmarie and Pearl into the classroom, Dr. Werner had spoken to Mrs. Gillpin in the hall privately. When Mrs. Gillpin returned to class she said nothing, but the slight shake of her head in disapproval was enough to tear at Jeanmarie's heart. They'd found out about Mr. Ripple, but guilt weighed heavy inside her for all the trouble she'd brought on not just herself but Pearl too. On the paper in front of her she began jotting down words for Dr. Werner's essay.

At supper Jeanmarie stole a long look at Mrs. Ripple, or Miss Ripple, if that's what she was now. Sympathy rolled over her. Her own mother and father didn't get along. Jeanmarie closed her eyes for grace. "Please, God, take care of Mrs. Ripple. Whatever her husband wants make him go away," she prayed silently. She'd said "Mrs. Ripple" out of habit.

While Pearl stood watch upstairs, Winnie fed the baby sparrow by hand as the others looked on. The little fellow seemed to understand what to do and ate greedily. "There now, enough for tonight," Winnie said. Jeanmarie stood on an upturned coal skuttle, and Winnie lifted the box up to her. Safely back on the ledge and camouflaged with the burlap rag the box seemed well hidden.

Pearl hadn't been idle. When the others came upstairs she beckoned them into the empty kitchen. "It's the ring; I've been thinking about Mrs. Ripple's wedding ring."

"But she doesn't have one," Tess objected. "That's strange, isn't it? Don't widows keep wearing their wedding rings?"

"Poor Mrs. Ripple isn't a widow. She might even be divorced, and why would she wear a wedding ring from the man she wanted to forget?" Jeanmarie said.

"Exactly," Pearl stated. "She might not wear it, but where is it?"

"I don't know," Winnie answered in an awed voice.

"Even if she didn't wear it, she'd want to keep it, right? What if it's in the change purse that's missing?" Pearl said. "And along comes Mr. Ripple wanting money, and when she doesn't have it, he wants the ring back. To sell it most likely. And Mrs. Ripple doesn't have it. Maybe that's why she felt so awful the night you heard her crying, Jem; the ring was missing." Pearl had thought it through thoroughly.

Jeanmarie gripped Pearl's arm. "Brilliant. And I'm sure I know where it is. The box in Sophie's drawer. No wonder she's taped it so tightly." A picture of Sophie standing next to Wilfred holding their winning art project together flitted before her. "It's Sophie alright. I knew it from the beginning. That box is proof. We find the wedding ring, and we find our thief. We have no choice but to open the box."

"Remember the letters," Winnie said softly. "Sophie didn't write the letters."

"And my charm bracelet," Maria said. "Maybe it's in the box too."

Maria's face looked so wistful, Jeanmarie reached out and patted her arm. "I'm positive she's our thief even if the letters didn't come from her," she said stubbornly. "There's no one else. And we know guilt can make a person sleepwalk. Sophie sleepwalks."

TWELVE

Runaway

On Friday a beaming Mrs. Gillpin announced that the orphanage now had its own library. "Class, Dr. Werner has informed me that thanks to some kind donors we are the privileged owners of enough books for a small library. He has allowed us a room next door to his office. I know you will all want to participate."

Mrs. Gillpin stood proudly at the door as the class entered the small windowless room now converted to a library. The shelves against the wall were filled with books, most of them well used, Jeanmarie thought, from the looks of their covers. Beside her, Pearl lovingly touched the back of a thick copy of *Grimms' Fairy Tales*. Her face bore a look of awe as she said softly, "So many books, and we can take any of them."

"But you only have ten minutes to decide which one," Jeanmarie teased. All of them knew Pearl would rather read than do most anything else. "Why don't we each take something both of us want to read, and we can swap." Pearl looked pleased at the idea. Since only one book was allowed to a person it would give them each two. Holding her own choice—*Oliver Twist*—carefully, Pearl nodded approval to Jeanmarie's *The Call of the Wild*. Jeanmarie had read it once, but it was the kind of book that begged to be read again, and she could hardly wait to begin.

While Mrs. Gillpin closed and locked the library door, Jeanmarie walked slowly back to class with the others. A tug on her arm made her turn to look. "Leah, hi." Leah's face was better except for a few scabs from the poison ivy, and her hands too were almost clear. Her thin hair looked duller than ever around her plain face. Quiet as a shadow in a bony frame, Leah didn't talk much, and Jeanmarie searched her eyes for some sign of what she wanted.

"Got something for you," Leah said, holding a stamp between her fingers. "Heard you needed one. Here, take it. I owe you. You and Sophie both. I don't know what I'd a done when the poison ivy was so bad. Take it; it's okay. I don't need it anyway."

Jeanmarie took the stamp before she could help herself. "Thanks," she murmured. "Sophie? Did you say me and Sophie?"

Leah grinned. "You know you helped me out that night with the witch hazel and all. Sophie too. Next best thing to two angels, you two." Leah slipped away, having said as many words as she was likely ever to say at one time.

Sophie? Back in class Jeanmarie stole a look at Sophie. With her head lowered above the book on her desk her red hair screened part of her face. Across the way Wilfred pushed his glasses back on his nose. Sophie glanced up and smiled at him. Jeanmarie turned away quickly. Whatever Sophie's scheme was, Wilfred didn't suspect a thing. No one else had ever outdone Wilfred in class before. He was the class brain, plain old Wilfred, the brain. If he didn't make an effort Sophie would be the class valedictorian come June. Jeanmarie was sure he was letting Sophie get ahead of him deliberately. Hadn't he made a foolish mistake when just the two of them were left in the spelling bee? Sophie had won. Maybe Sophie was Leah's angel, but then the worst criminal might still have some good spot. She'd heard that Hitler liked young children so long as they weren't Jewish.

A soft swish caught her attention in time to take the note Pearl carefully passed behind her into Jeanmarie's palm. "Where did L. get that stamp? S." Pearl always signed her notes S for Skinny as her alias. Jeanmarie turned it over and wrote, "Don't know." Until now she hadn't given a thought to where Leah had come up with a stamp. Maybe Sophie had given it to her? Jeanmarie scribbled Sop.? on the note and sent it back to Pearl. If Leah knew something that could help them catch Sophie, they'd better find out tonight.

Light still glowed in the sky as Jeanmarie hurried from the farmhouse. The air felt unusually warm, more like summer than early spring. She would like to have searched the ice-cold brook on the meadow side of the road for clumps of black frog's eggs that felt like thick jelly when you held them, but not tonight.

Inside Wheelock Cottage dining room two girls hurried to finish setting tables for the supper meal. In the kitchen Sophie left her sopping wet apron in the laundry sink. In spite of the apron a large stain spread across her skirt where spilled juice had leaked through.

Mrs. Ripple shook her head. "You'd better run upstairs and change. You'll need to soak that skirt too. We'll take care of things here." Sophie left the kitchen. She hadn't meant to spill the juice, but the heavy pitcher had slipped, pouring most of its contents on her and the floor. She supposed she would be punished.

In the small dorm Maria laid the book she had chosen to read to Lizzie and the rest of the little girls on Lizzie's bed. She glanced up as Sophie ran into the room and stripped off her skirt. "Accident?" Maria inquired.

Sophie answered briefly, "Spilled juice." As she began rolling up the skirt something shiny tumbled from its pocket.

Before Sophie could bend to retrieve it Maria swooped it up. "That's my charm bracelet. You stole my charm bracelet." Maria's voice rose as her words poured out. "It was you all along stealing from us. And I even defended you and said it couldn't be you." Angry tears threatened to spill. "I don't know what you've done with all the rest of the stuff you took, but you'd better give it back. Mrs. Ripple's change purse and everything."

White-faced, Sophie stood with her wet skirt in her hands. "I found that bracelet. I never stole from you or anyone."

"Then why didn't you give it back? What was it doing in your pocket? You know where lost things are supposed to go. You're lying just like you did about your folks. You've lied all along." Maria's eyes flashed.

Dropping the wet skirt on the floor, Sophie pulled open her dresser drawer and grabbed a fresh one. Banging the drawer shut she faced Maria. "I don't care what you believe. I didn't steal your old bracelet or anything else." Quickly she pushed past Maria and fled into the small bathroom.

With her back against the door to hold it shut, Sophie put on her skirt as tears streamed down her face. "I should have told her the truth. But she wouldn't believe it anyway." They were all against her. Like a wilted flower she slumped to the floor, her back still pressed tightly against the door. They all thought she was a thief. They'd been talking behind her back all this time and pretending to be friendly. Was Leah in on it too?

Sophie listened for footsteps but heard none. Downstairs Mrs. Ripple was ringing the bell for supper; Sophie didn't move. The minutes passed slowly. By now everyone was in the dining room eating. Carefully she opened the door. The only noise came from below in the direction of the dining room. Sophie crept quietly to the stairway. Satisfied that no one would hear her she went downstairs. Keeping close to the wall she slipped quietly into the hallway to the cellar door. Once inside the cellar she knew what she must do.

The day had been warm, but she would take her jacket with her. She slipped it from its hook and stood with it over her arm. A fluttering sound made her turn toward the furnace. Days ago she'd discovered the baby sparrow's box behind the burlap rag when she'd grown curious at a chirping sound behind the furnace. At first she'd thought it was a cricket. A strong desire to see it one more time moved her. The tiny thing seemed glad to see her as she lifted its box down.

"Poor thing. If you could fly I'd set you free. I wish I could take you with me, but it's a long way back to the city, and I don't even know if I can find the old tailor shop by myself. If I do I'll beg them to take me in. I'm strong, and I can work." The bird moved its head sideways, eyeing her. "At least you listen," Sophie said. "In you go now. I'll miss you." Gently she replaced the bird, put the box on the shelf, and draped it from sight with the burlap. "So long. Get well soon," she whispered. Without looking back she quietly opened the cellar door and stepped out into the night.

Mrs. Ripple had no sooner finished saying grace when Maria held the charm bracelet up for the others at the table to see. "It was Sophie," she whispered. "I caught her with it myself."

Jeanmarie looked quickly across the room to Sophie's table, but she wasn't in her place. "Where is she? What did she say?" she demanded.

All eyes were on Maria as she explained, adding at the end, "But she still denies everything."

"Guess we should have expected she would," Jeanmarie said. A feeling that Sophie might never admit anything nagged at her. "She won't dare take anything more now that she knows we're on to her, but that won't bring back the things she took."

"And there's still the change purse and what's in it," Pearl reminded them.

With a sigh Jeanmarie leaned back against her chair. "The question is, what do we do next?" It was Mrs. Ripple who answered it. Supper ended, and still Sophie didn't appear. Mrs. Ripple had gone to find her, but Sophie seemed to have disappeared.

"Girls, have any of you seen Sophie?" An anxious look creased Mrs. Ripple's forehead. No one knew where Sophie might be. Mrs. Ripple paled when a thorough search of the house revealed that Sophie was indeed missing. "I don't want to call Dr. Werner just yet," she said. "Being at the orphanage is still new to Sophie, and it's possible that she just decided to go for a walk by herself. She may have felt bad about spilling the juice before supper and needed to be alone for a while. Let's see if we can find her ourselves." A chorus of voices volunteering rang out.

"Good," she said. "Leah, you take charge of the younger girls in the game room, and I'll join you as soon as I can." With Leah and the children gone, the only ones left were Jeanmarie, the twins, Pearl, and Winnie. All of the older girls were at a special event at the high school. "Girls," Mrs. Ripple began, "two of you can search the gardens and yard while the other three take a look up the hill past the rest of the girls' cottages. She may have walked that way. I don't think she would go down toward Dr. Werner's. When you find her tell her I would like her to return please. Her supper is waiting in the kitchen. You might add, whichever of you finds her first, that we've all spilled a few things around here, and now she's really one of us." Mrs. Ripple smiled. "I think we can do this without bothering the administration. Let's try, shall we? I will be right here waiting for you, girls, and praying," she added.

Outside the night air felt warm for early spring. A full moon shone brightly. Jeanmarie stood in a little group with the others. "We can start out back, but why don't we all stick together to cover it? That way we can make sure we don't miss anything." Sophie was not in the garden or the small clump of trees and bushes that ran between it and the road. All along, Jeanmarie had known they wouldn't find her there. "I think she's run away," she announced.

"Poor thing," Winnie exclaimed, her voice sounding sympathetic.

Maria stuck her chin out. "You may be sorry for her, but I hope she's gone for good."

"Wait a minute," Pearl said. "Let's not forget that we have to find her if we're ever going to get back Mrs. Ripple's ring or whatever was in that change purse. If she's running, then there goes the purse too and who knows what else. And don't forget Mr. Ripple. There's no telling what threats he's already made."

Jeanmarie nodded. "You're right. We have to find her for Mrs. Ripple's sake." A plan already forming in her mind, she took charge. "Sophie doesn't know the area like we do, but she must have seen the old migrant place down by the railroad tracks and the orchard tower. She might be hiding out in either of those two, or she could have decided to follow the tracks. It isn't likely she'd just walk along the road where someone could spot her. Winnie, why don't you go with Tess and Maria and check out the house. Pearl, you could check the tower, while I take a look along the tracks away from town." Agreeing, they were about to split, when Jeanmarie thought of one thing more.

"We should have a signal. Whoever finds her better signal for the rest of us to come. We need something others won't pay attention to, like 'Ally, Ally, in free.'" It was the call they used in hide-and-seek to bring the players home when someone was found.

As Jeanmarie made her way onto the tracks she glanced wistfully up at the nearby orchard where Pearl had already disappeared into the shadows. Thanks to the bright moonlight she could see ahead a good ways to where the tracks curved out of sight; still, she did wish they'd thought to bring flashlights.

Jeanmarie knew these tracks well. If Sophie followed them she would be able to see her once she'd passed the first and second bend. Of course she could be hiding somewhere in the thick brush on either side. A small animal scurried close to the tracks, and Jeanmarie peered at the shadowy bush that soon swallowed it from sight. She shivered as a great owl flew low overhead and into a clump of trees close by. If Sophie was out here alone and frightened she might be ready to go back. Just loud enough so as not to scare her off, she called, "Sophie; it's me—Jeanmarie. Don't be scared; it's just me. Sophie . . ."

THIRTEEN

A Headlong Fall

Sophie had one goal—get back to the city and find her father's old friend, Herman the tailor. Her only hope of getting there was the train track. The track lay deserted in the moonlight. If she followed it faithfully it should eventually lead her right to the city. But if she went south the police or whoever the orphanage sent to find her might think the same thing she was thinking—New York City—and be on the lookout.

Longingly Sophie looked at the smooth tracks and imagined herself gliding along them straight home. On the other hand, what if she headed north first? North meant small towns and fewer railroad stations. Maybe she'd even be able to find a way to ride the train back. With the war on and everyone working for the war effort someone might take pity on her. She could make up a story that she'd lost her ticket and was supposed to be on her way to meet her soldier papa just back from the army. She swallowed hard and stepped toward the tracks. Quickly she withdrew her foot. She didn't know for sure, but wasn't one of the rails electric and certain death if you touched it? She would have to walk between the rails. Gingerly she stepped inside.

If it hadn't been for the ominous sounds from creatures Sophie couldn't see and night birds that startled her every now and then, she could have walked in the narrow strip beside the tracks. At first she tried skipping one cross tie to reach the next, but the space between them was too large. Touching down on every cross tie made her steps too small, but it would have to do. It also slowed her down.

Past the first curve of the tracks she decided to walk on the left of the tracks, at least for a while. As she stepped onto the strip, thick overgrown bushes scratched at her legs, forcing her to inch closer to the rail. At the same time her fear that this might be the deadly rail made her want to stay as far as possible from it. Caught between the two, she wondered if maybe she ought to explore the other side of the bushes and see if the walking was better there. So long as she kept the tracks on her right, at least the bushes that bordered them would guide her. She would make her way through the bushes just ahead.

Stamping her feet first to frighten away any small animals, Sophie pushed into the bushes. Prickles caught her hair and clung to her legs and hands, even her jacket. Untangling herself seemed hopeless; panicked, she pulled and tore her way through with all her strength, at last pitching forward, free of the briars. A strangled cry broke from her throat. She was falling, plunging headlong down a steep bank, along with stones and clumps of dirt rushing with her.

Icy cold water covered her head and filled her mouth, choking her, swallowing her. Her arms flailed as she struggled. Her clothing clung to her, and her shoes were heavy weights. Inside, a voice like her mother's urged her, "Swim, Sophie, swim." She managed to kick her way back to the surface. Gasping for air she kept her head free of the water; using her feet she pried off first one shoe and then the other. Freed from the extra weight she tried to get her bearings. She had fallen into some kind of deep pit with water in it. How far down the water reached she didn't know, but her feet were not touching bottom. "Help! Somebody help!" she cried. Stillness filled the shadows above the edges of the pit. She knew there was no one around, but she called again and again. What if no one ever came this way? A sob caught in her throat. "Please, God . . . help me." Frantic, Sophie searched the sloping sides of the pit for some way out.

The side to her left seemed to slope more than the others. If she could just find a handhold or a foothold she could climb it. She swam toward the slope. What else was in the icy water? The thought made her kick faster. As she neared the side she felt below her for the bottom. Nothing. Above her and beyond her reach the slope began, but with nothing to stand on or hang onto she couldn't reach it. "I could drag myself up that slope if I could just get to it," she said aloud.

She would have to tread water until she found a way. But how long could she hold out? She was already tired. Her hands dug into the hard earth on the side of the pit, but each time they slipped off. Her fingers were now raw from their clawing. Sophie lost track of time as she let her face sink into the water and let her body hang motionless; then she picked up to breathe and fluttered her hands enough to keep herself afloat. Over and over she repeated the motions the way her mother had taught her long ago. Was it hours since she'd fallen into the pit?

Jeanmarie neared the curve of the track. After that the tracks ran straight for a long way. If she didn't see anything ahead, she would turn back and go south. Dutifully she called, "Sophie, are you here? Sophie, it's just me—Jeanmarie." Would Sophie answer even if she heard?

Rounding the curve Jeanmarie saw in the bright moonlight that the tracks beyond were clear. Nothing! She might as well turn back. Planting her feet wide she gave one more call in her loudest tone: "Sophie! If you are anywhere around here you better say so. This is your last chance. Mrs. Ripple sent us out to bring you back. You needn't have left in the first place. We've all spilled stuff in our time. Do you hear me?" Of course Sophie didn't hear her; nobody did. Why in the world had she said all that? She turned to head back.

"Help; help me! Somebody help me! Help; help!" The cries came from right near the tracks. Jeanmarie turned quickly. The only thing on that side was the old railroad swimming hole, the one Dr. Werner had forbidden them to go near. It wasn't really a swimming hole, just a deep pit with water in it. Sophie! Was she in the pit?

Jeanmarie knew the path around the pit and headed to it, calling as she went. "Sophie, is that you? I'm coming. It's me—Jeanmarie." Her heart raced as she pushed her way toward the edge of the pit. The cries for help were definitely coming from there. In spite of the bright moonlight she could barely make out the figure at the bottom as she peered down. "Sophie, is that you? Hang on; it's me—Jeanmarie."

"Yes, it's me!" Sophie wailed. "I can't keep up much longer. I'm so cold. Please help me!"

Jeanmarie looked around her for something to use but saw nothing. There was no way she could get down there. "I have to go for help!" she cried. "I can't reach you without a rope."

"No, don't leave me," Sophie begged. "I'll die by myself; please don't leave me here."

Jeanmarie's stomach lurched. What should she do? "I won't leave you, Sophie, but we need help," she called. "The others are looking for you too—in the orchard and at the old migrant house. By now they know you aren't there. I told them I'd look along the tracks. We agreed on a signal, so hold on, please." Cupping her hands around her mouth Jeanmarie shouted, "Ally, Ally, in free," waited, and shouted again. No one answered. Twice more she tried without response. Maybe they just couldn't hear her. She leaned over the edge and called to Sophie, "Hang on; please hang on!"

"I can't keep up," Sophie cried. Her voice sounded thin and shaky.

Jeanmarie tried to comfort her. "They'll be here anytime now. They'll come looking for me when I don't show up. They know I'm here searching the tracks." What she didn't tell Sophie was that she hadn't told them she'd be heading north. They were probably looking for her on the tracks going south. No wonder they hadn't heard her signal. She had to do something and quickly. "Please, God, help us. We don't know what to do, and Sophie can't hold on much longer." An idea formed in her mind. Sophie needed something to hold her! But what?

"Sophie!" she called down. "I've got an idea. Wait just a few minutes more, okay?"

Quickly Jeanmarie hurried from the pit toward the nearest clump of trees. Stomping her feet to frighten away any unwanted company, she searched the shadows, looking for a fallen tree limb or something big enough to help. What she wanted lay close to a large tree. Broken off from its ancient parent tree the thick limb was almost too heavy for her. She dragged it over to the pit by the smaller end. The thing was at least five feet long. This wouldn't be easy, and it could be dangerous for Sophie down below.

"Listen to me, Sophie," she called. "I'm going to slide a log down the slope into the water, but you have to stay out of the way. You need to flatten yourself against the pit away from the sloping side, and don't move until I tell you. Can you do that?"

Sophie's voice was eager. "Yes, I'm doing it." A moment later, she called back, "Ready! But hurry; there's nothing to hold onto."

"Just don't move," Jeanmarie ordered. "Ready? Alright, here goes." Jeanmarie had slid the log over the edge so it would slide down the slope the rest of the way, and with a great push she sent it down. The log hit with a smacking sound. Jeanmarie felt her heart beat wildly. "Sophie; Sophie, are you okay?" she cried.

For a few minutes sounds of splashing reached her and then a voice: "I've got it!" In the water Sophie clung to the floating log. She didn't dare try to sit on it, but with her shoulders and head resting on it and her arms wrapped around it, she rested and let her legs dangle. After a bit she dared to look up. Jeanmarie was still there at the edge of the pit.

"The others will be coming soon," Jeanmarie called. "Are you okay?" she asked anxiously. For all she knew Sophie might be hurt from her fall into the pit.

"Thanks," Sophie replied in a weary voice. "If I ever get out of here I'll owe my life to you."

Jeanmarie pursed her lips. This was no time to be reminded that Sophie did owe her and all of them. Instead she leaned over and said, "What would I do with two lives anyway? If there were two of me I think Dr. Werner would resign. After tonight, he might. Just kidding." Jeanmarie needed to keep Sophie talking and hanging on until help arrived. "Sophie, where'd you learn to swim?" she asked. It was a silly question, but it was all Jeanmarie could think of at the moment.

Sounds in the distance alerted them both. The others were coming! In moments Pearl and Tess were running as fast as they'd ever run back to the orphanage for help. Winnie and Maria stayed with Jeanmarie. Tears streamed down Winnie's face, and Maria held her hand as the three of them watched the frail, shadowy figure below cling to the log that was keeping her from certain drowning.

FOURTEEN

A Rescue and a Burial

As the rescue team worked near the edge of the pit, Jeanmarie and the others strained to see from several feet away where they'd been told to stay put. Once Dr. Werner glanced at them; then he turned to help the five volunteer firemen and two policemen with the equipment and heavy ropes. Dr. Werner's words when he'd first seen Jeanmarie peering into the pit were not new to her. "You," he'd said. "I might have guessed." It was what he always said when she was in trouble, but this time she felt their sting go deeply. Of course, Mrs. Ripple hadn't told her to search the tracks, but for Sophie's sake she was glad she had.

With the young men off to the war it was older men who filled the jobs at home, and Jeanmarie held her breath as the men worked to lower one of the volunteers into the pit. In a few moments she heard the call from below: "All set!" As she watched, the men pulled up a second rope with a small chair attached to it and strapped in it a white-faced Sophie.

Back in Wheelock the doctor had come and gone. Jeanmarie waited with the others in the game room for Dr. Werner and Mrs. Ripple, who were still upstairs with Sophie. Every voice hushed as heavy footsteps descended the stairs. Across from Jeanmarie, Maria looked as if she would faint any moment. "It's all my fault," Maria whispered. Dr. Werner, followed by Mrs. Ripple, came to the doorway of the game room.

The look on Dr. Werner's face grew stern. "You will all take note of the consequences of such behavior as running off without permission. Not only do you endanger your own life and limb but those of others who may have to rescue you." He looked directly at Jeanmarie. "As for you, young lady, whether it was your sober reasoning or your impetuous instinct that led you to Sophie I am not sure. But did it not occur to you to ask Mrs. Ripple's permission to search the tracks? You might have fallen into the pit yourself unknown to the others, and then what would have happened to Sophie? Or yourself? You must learn to think, Jeanmarie." He paused, then went on. "We may thank God there was no drowning tonight. I shall expect no further disruptions." With a final nod to Mrs. Ripple he left. Jeanmarie couldn't believe it! Dr. Werner hadn't said a word about Sophie and Maria's bracelet. He must not know!

Mrs. Ripple, pale and teary-eyed, came into the room and sat. "Dr. Werner is right. Sophie could have drowned." She looked directly at Jeanmarie and Pearl and at the twins and Winnie who were sitting with them. "Though Dr. Werner is quite correct and going beyond the boundaries without permission must not be, still you meant well, girls, and thanks to you Sophie is safe. The doctor says that keeping her warm and in bed for a few days will take care of the chills as well as her sprained foot. It saddens me to think that any of you girls would feel so alone and so frightened that you would want to run away. It must have been something more than the spilled juice that made Sophie feel so bad. I don't believe she thinks of this as her home yet, and I'm afraid some of that is my fault. I've been letting other things occupy my thoughts far too much. Now, do you think we can all make a real effort to help Sophie know we want her here?" Several voiced their agreement, especially among the younger girls, like Lizzie, who immediately offered to play with her.

Jeanmarie looked at Pearl and the others. Maria's eyes were glistening, but were they tears of sympathy or frustration? Now what? Even if Sophie decided to make a change for the better, what about the missing things? The change purse and ring?

When they'd finally settled down for the night, Pearl called softly across the room, "I forgot tomorrow is Saturday, and I've got another appointment with the dentist. I have to be there in the afternoon again."

Jeanmarie heard her groan. "It's okay," she said. "Mrs. Shapiro always understands." She turned on her side and plumped the pillow. "I guess it will be just me, since Sophie won't be going this time," she added. Thanks to her near drowning, Sophie wasn't going anywhere soon. At least I won't have to watch her every minute at work, Jeanmarie thought, remembering Sophie and the menorah. A picture of Sophie struggling to stay afloat in the deep railroad pit flashed before her. What if she had drowned? Guilt nagged at Jeanmarie's heart. Maybe if she'd talked Dutch Uncle—straight to her—about the thefts Sophie might have confessed.

For a minute Jeanmarie's thoughts wandered to the storefront church back in Harlem where as a little girl she went to hear Mother Anderson preach. Mother Anderson was strict about stealing and lying, but she was even stronger on confessing your sins. Maybe a good dose of Mother Anderson would've done Sophie some good. Jeanmarie began to pray. "Dear God, thanks for not letting Sophie drown. I guess you give a lot of second chances. I'll try to do better, but sometimes it's hard being an orphan." She paused; she wasn't a real orphan. "I guess you could say I've been here so long I'm practically an orphan," she added. Satisfied, she felt the familiar blanket of sleep stealing over her, and she closed her eyes. Tomorrow was Saturday, another workday.

Jeanmarie arrived at work early. Mrs. Shapiro murmured in sympathy as she led Jeanmarie to the kitchen. By the time she left work there was still no sign of David though his grandmother had come as usual. The bag of cookies from Mrs. Shapiro wouldn't fit into Jeanmarie's pocket so she held it in the crook of her arm. Where the path met the road and the woods were thick she stopped to open the bag. Before she could untwist the top of it something caught her attention. Close to where she stood a thicket of maple trees and low-growing bushes bordered the road. She thought she heard sounds coming from that direction.

Gripping the bag of cookies tightly she edged toward the sound. Moaning—that was what she heard. Boldly, Jeanmarie went closer, staying behind the shelter of bushes until she came to the place. Slowly at first, and then with a rush, what she saw became clear to her. In a small clearing between the trees, David knelt rocking and crying. A small mound of dirt in front of him held a broken bird's nest that looked as if someone had tried to put it back together. Next to it lay a hockey stick she had seen back at the Shapiros'.

She had come upon him so suddenly that he had no time to run. Tears still streaked his face as he cried out, "I didn't mean to do it; I didn't."

In an instant Jeanmarie found herself kneeling on the ground next to him, anger flooding her as she gripped his arm and shook him. "You broke all those nests with the hockey stick. You killed the baby birds. How could you do such a terrible thing?" she demanded. She was still shaking him as David threw his arms up in front of his face to defend himself. Barely knowing what she had done, Jeanmarie stopped, let go of his arm, and sat back. David cried loudly, his hands still in front of his face.

Jeanmarie hadn't meant to shake him so hard. "You better stop crying," she ordered, "and tell me why you did this."

Gradually, David's wailing lessened. After a few gulps he peered at her from between his fingers, then let his hands drop. Not looking at her, he said in a low voice, "I was playing soldiers, and the nests just got in the way. I didn't mean to hurt the baby birds, only the eggs." He looked at her now, his eyes pleading for understanding. "It just happened," he said.

"Soldiers don't go around knocking down bird's nests and killing baby birds," she snapped.

Before her eyes David lost control. "They do; they do. They kill Jewish children and old people too. I know they do," he cried. Still on his knees he rocked back and forth, his small hands once more covering his face, his little voice wailing loudly.

Horrified, Jeanmarie realized he meant the Nazis. "David, David," she said, trying to calm him. "You were playing Nazis? David, you mustn't." She leaned closer to him. "Don't you know God will punish them? Our soldiers are fighting right now to end the war and stop the evil. Oh, David." She reached to touch him half afraid but wanting to stop the awful rocking.

Slowly David stopped until he sat still. His eyes, heavy with grief, met hers. "Will God punish me for the birds?" he whispered.

Jeanmarie felt tears filling her own eyes and spilling over. "David, you buried the birds didn't you?" David nodded. "And you're sorry. We're both sad. I think God knows how we feel. Why don't we say a prayer over them?"

"You mean Kaddish?" David asked. "I don't know if you can say that for birds; it's a prayer for dead people."

"Then why don't I pray this time?" Jeanmarie offered. She held David's hands tightly. "Dear Father God, we feel so sad about the baby birds and the eggs that won't ever be robins now. Please forgive us. And God, please let the war end soon. Amen."

David wiped his eyes as Jeanmarie stood. "Come on, David; it's time to go home," she said. "Do you want your stick?"

"Could you carry it back?" David asked. "I don't want it anymore."

Jeanmarie wiped her own eyes and took David's hand. Under her other arm she carried the cookies and the stick. "Have a cookie?" she offered. Together they walked to the Shapiros'. Close to the cottage she laid the hockey stick in the yard. "I'll see you next week," she said, patting David's arm. From the path she glanced back and waved. David lifted his hand, then turned and went inside the cottage.

Jeanmarie opened the bag in her hand and took out a cookie. She thought of the pictures Mrs. Gillpin had showed them in the *New York Times* of Jewish people rescued by the Allies from terrible places called concentration camps. They were like the ones in the newsreels, men and women so skinny they looked like children, nearly starved to death. Mrs. Gillpin explained that they'd been punished just for being Jewish. The pictures made Jeanmarie sick in her stomach. Pictures like those were enough to frighten any little Jewish child, like David, if he'd seen them. She reached into the bag for another cookie and found it empty. She hadn't even noticed how many she'd eaten. The sound of a vehicle behind her made her step off the road. Her throat tightened at the sight of the farmer's truck.

The small truck slowed to a stop directly in front of Jeanmarie. It was not the farmer but his thin little wife. The woman reached across to the passenger side and opened the door. "Hi; why don't you hop in, and I'll take you the rest of the way," she offered.

Jeanmarie hesitated, but when the woman smiled she felt that she ought to accept her offer, so she climbed in. "Thanks," she said. "I'm a little later than usual coming home, so the ride will be great." Jeanmarie's face burned. Should she ask about Ralph? Though she hadn't thought of him at all lately, suddenly here was his mother, and all she could think about now was Ralph.

"Been off grounds working, I take it," the farmer's wife said. "Pretty alongside the road here now that we've had some good growing weather. Ralph, my boy, used to like to hike these woods."

Jeanmarie stole a look at the woman. Her eyes were on the road ahead, but she turned slightly and glanced at Jeanmarie as though waiting for her to say something. "I know Ralph; who he is, I mean. How is he?" Jeanmarie asked.

The woman's voice was low and sad as she answered. "He's gone off, you know. Maybe you didn't know that. I don't suppose you ever heard him mention where he might be headed? Seems like he hung around some with the boys at the orphanage, but they don't know where he might be off to. He's too young to join up with the army. Anyway, we checked it out, and no one's seen him." For a moment the woman looked searchingly at Jeanmarie.

Should she tell her about Ralph? Jeanmarie was sure her own face betrayed her. She swallowed hard.

"I'm his mother. I have a right to know," the woman cried, adding with a low voice full of pain, "I'm so sorry. It's just that I need to know he's alright."

Jeanmarie's eyes filled with tears. "The only thing I can tell you is that Ralph did say he wanted to be a veterinarian like his uncle Joe. He may have gone to live with him."

The woman looked at Jeanmarie, then back at the road. "His uncle Joe," she said softly. "Ralph's a good boy, always trying to please his pa, but his pa's so set on him being a big farmer, he won't hear of anything else. I should have known. Ever since Ralph was a little tyke he had a liking for animals, all kinds." Her voice seemed to lighten as if with hope. "He'll be alright then, once he gets to his uncle's." They arrived at the orphanage grounds, and the farmer's wife stopped the car. "Bless you, child," she said as Jeanmarie thanked her and got out.

Back at Wheelock Jeanmarie remembered she still had to do her weekly laundry. "You too?" Pearl said, putting a large bundle next to Jeanmarie's on the floor by the laundry tubs. They'd barely finished by the time supper was ready. Afterward Pearl had gone to read to the younger girls, and Jeanmarie went upstairs. It had been a long day.

Jeanmarie reached for her diary and undid the metal clasp. For a long while she sat thinking. At last she wrote, "I don't know why there's so many hard things in this world. Like Ralph running away when he's got a mother who loves him, and here's a whole orphanage full of kids who don't have a real home." The idea came back to her that if she hadn't been so mean to Ralph he might not have run away. She didn't write that down but instead wrote, "Poor David." She finished writing and set the diary in her lap.

What if something terrible happened to Ralph and he never made it to his uncle Joe's? It would be all her fault. But wasn't his father to blame for his terrible temper too and for not listening to Ralph? She hadn't listened either. Ralph tried to explain to her about his father the day before he'd run away. She had done everything but clap her hands over her ears to not listen to him. Guilt like a heavy blanket wrapped around her. "Please forgive me, God," she began and stopped abruptly. Words she'd learned long ago popped into her mind: "If you don't forgive others, your heavenly Father won't forgive you your trespasses." Ralph's father? She hadn't forgiven him for nearly running her down. She hoped God would understand.

The light outside faded and night fell before Jeanmarie rose and put her diary away. As she stooped to replace her keepsake box under the nightstand, she remembered the face of Ralph's mother. Tears filled her eyes. Mothers shouldn't have to do all the suffering. Guilt still nagged at her. It wasn't fair! She wiped her eyes as the voices and laughter of the younger girls on their way upstairs reached her.

FIFTEEN

Mr. Ripple Pays a Visit

A weak spring sun failed to warm the rock Jeanmarie was sitting on; she had a notebook on her lap, with the letter she had just finished writing tucked into it. A letter from her mother lay folded in her pocket. She'd read the single paragraph over and over until she knew it by heart: "Dear Jeanmarie, how are you? The rooming house here is not too bad, but the assembly line gets tiring day after day doing the same thing. Oh well, it's all for the war effort. I wish I could have stayed longer at the last factory, but you know I have to keep moving. One of these days everything will be okay. Don't forget to write. You mustn't give this address to your father. I have to go; second shift starts soon. Just call me Rosie the Riveter. Love you, Mom." Jeanmarie smiled. Rosie the Riveter was one of the famous poster girls showing what women were doing for the war effort these days.

If her father did visit, of course she wouldn't let him see the letter. Not that her mom stayed long at any address. Thank goodness she had that stamp from Leah. If she mailed her letter right away chances were her mom would still be there. The stamp! In a panic she jumped to her feet. The stamp had been there this morning, but what if it was gone by now? Why didn't I put it in my pocket when I had the chance, she wailed to herself. Clutching the notebook to her chest she ran blindly out of the small wooded area, through the yard, and around the corner of the cottage.

The notebook flew out of her arms as she collided with a man who uttered a loud "Ooph." For a moment the stranger held her. When he released her she stepped back. "Not you again," he said. Horrified, Jeanmarie saw that it was the same man in the same dark raincoat, the man she'd crashed into a week ago.

The man straightened the front of his raincoat. His face was younger than Jeanmarie remembered. "Do you make a habit of running into people?" he asked. "Or is it that you just run instead of walk? I suppose you're all right?" He looked at Jeanmarie for a moment. "Well then, since you've no visible wounds and nothing to say I'll be off. Better watch yourself, young lady." He walked away in the direction of the road, limping as he went, heading for a small car parked at the side of the orchard road.

Jeanmarie swallowed hard. She'd managed to bump into the same man twice. What was he doing here? She bent to pick up her notebook with the precious letter still inside it. By the time she straightened, Winnie came bounding down the steps.

"You missed him," Winnie said breathlessly. "He was here; Mr. Ripple was right here."

"You mean the man in the dark raincoat?" she asked breathlessly. "That's Mrs. Ripple's husband? The man I just ran into?"

Winnie's eyes grew wide. "You ran into him? I let him in less than half an hour ago. He came to the door asking for Mrs. Ripple, and I said, 'Who should I tell her is calling?' He said bold as could be, 'Tell her Mr. Ripple is here.' When I told her, Mrs. Ripple came right to the door and took him straight upstairs to her room. That's all I know. But it was him for a fact."

Jeanmarie stared at Winnie. Mr. Ripple! Awe filled her. "He was here once before, Win. That's the very same man I told you all about, the one I ran into. What was he doing here?" So Pearl hadn't heard a radio program that night. It was Mr. Ripple she'd heard, and he had been coming out of the house when Jeanmarie bumped into him!

Winnie's soft voice ventured, "Maybe he's come to plead with her to go back with him. We all saw him. He didn't look like a terrible man."

Jeanmarie cleared her throat. "Win, they don't always look evil, the scoundrels I mean. He's younger than I thought he'd be, that's for sure. At least now we know who we're dealing with." Winnie nodded. "And, Win, remember he hasn't paid his hotel bill? Most likely that's what he's after—money." She hurried up the steps, Winnie following. "I just have to find my stamp," she said and added, "if it's still there. Then we'd better get the others together for a meeting."

The stamp lay where Jeanmarie had left it tucked into the corner of her drawer. With a sigh of relief she picked it up, licked it, and put it firmly on the front of the letter. She'd mail it tomorrow in Miss Bigler's office. The phone in the hallway rang, and Jeanmarie paused. Should she answer it? Before she could decide, Mrs. Ripple's footsteps hurried past the doorway. Jeanmarie couldn't help listening. After Mrs. Ripple's first words Jeanmarie strained to hear the rest.

"He was here today. . . . Yes, I will," Mrs. Ripple said to whoever was on the other end of the phone. "It's the only thing to do," she continued. "I can't give him what he wants. . . . No; there's nothing you can do to help right now. I should be seeing you soon. No; I don't plan to take much, just what will fit in a large suitcase."

Jeanmarie waited until Mrs. Ripple hung up and left. When she heard the door to her room close, she hurried into the hall and down the stairs. This was urgent. Mrs. Ripple was leaving the orphanage!

One by one she'd signaled the others to meet her in the cellar. In the corner of the furnace room near the baby sparrow's window box the five friends huddled together for a meeting. Jeanmarie exclaimed, "She's really leaving!" Carefully she repeated the phone call she'd overheard. "Her husband, or ex-husband, shows up today, and suddenly Mrs. Ripple is planning to go away." Pearl and the twins stared at her. "She said it was the only thing she could do," Jeanmarie added softly.

Winnie sniffled. "If only we'd known it was her husband, maybe we could have done something. I could have pretended she wasn't home." Winnie looked as if she would cry.

"Sooner or later, Win, he'd have found out the truth," Jeanmarie said, "and come for her no matter what."

"The scoundrel!" Maria exclaimed. "Poor Mrs. Ripple."

Pearl looked thoughtful. "We know he owes money to that rundown hotel, and he's the one behind those letters that upset her so much."

"And we know he's been here before at least once—the night I ran into him—and then again today. And we think he's called her too," Jeanmarie added.

"Right," Pearl agreed. "No wonder she's running away from him."

"It looks like she's running," Jeanmarie agreed. "I heard her say all she's taking is a large suitcase. At least she'll be safe with her family." Jeanmarie wasn't positive the person on the other end of the phone was a family member, but whoever it was, Mrs. Ripple trusted the person.

Tess asked anxiously, "Do you think he mistreated her?" A long silence followed. It was not impossible.

Jeanmarie cleared her throat. "We know he's up to no good. She never would have come here and not let anyone know she was married unless something was wrong."

Pearl said slowly, "She said on the phone, 'I can't give it to him,' and we know from the hotel clerk we called that he needs money. But suppose he knows that Mrs. Ripple doesn't have the money, and he came here to demand she give him back the wedding ring? A wedding ring can be worth a lot. He didn't look too happy when he left today, probably because he couldn't get what he wanted."

"Not if Mrs. Ripple doesn't have it because it was in her stolen change purse," Jeanmarie said. "Something about that change purse keeps coming back to me. None of us have ever even seen it. Mrs. Ripple never goes into town to shop. She orders things from the Sears catalogue. If she kept the ring in the purse, the thief might not even have known it was there until too late." The night Sophie'd walked in her sleep she'd gone straight into Mrs. Ripple's room, as if she'd been there before! Jeanmarie leaned toward the others, a plan already forming. "If we found the ring and sent it to Mr. Ripple at the hotel, he could sell it and keep the money. Maybe that's all he really wants."

Pearl clapped Jeanmarie on the shoulder. "We could write a note that this is the final word of warning and that the ring is his to use but he must never bother her again; then we could sign it 'A Friend.'"

"Oh, Pearl," Winnie said. "Do we dare?"

Tess held up her hand. "Aren't we forgetting something? We don't have the ring, and we don't have the missing change purse. How are we supposed to find them?"

Jeanmarie felt her face grow warm. "We don't know yet where the purse is. But I saw Sophie sleepwalk right into Mrs. Ripple's room, and we do know she has a taped-up box hidden in her drawer that's just right for a valuable ring."

All eyes now turned to Jeanmarie. "I know what you're thinking," she said. "Sophie nearly drowned running away, and we can't prove she stole Maria's charm bracelet. But if the ring's in the box in Sophie's drawer she won't be able to deny taking it." Jeanmarie knew she had all the proof she needed, but she didn't say it. "We have nothing to lose, and we have to do something to help Mrs. Ripple, and fast. I say we look in the box tonight."

"You mean open it on our own without Sophie?" Winnie asked.

"I guess we don't have any choice," Jeanmarie said softly.

"But how, when?" Pearl asked. "Who's going to risk taking the box right from under Sophie's nose?"

Jeanmarie rubbed her chin. With Sophie confined to bed with a strained foot, there was only one way. "I'll wait until everyone is asleep," she said. It would be like sleepwalking only she'd be awake.

At midnight Jeanmarie slipped quietly out of bed. Pearl had been awake first. "It's my inner clock," Pearl explained in a low voice. "I told myself I'd go with you, and here I am."

In the semidarkness Jeanmarie reached for Pearl's hand. "Thanks. I guess it's what best friends do," she said. "I'll go first in case somebody is awake."

Pearl made a sound somewhat like a chuckle. "And if they are I'll run back and pretend to be asleep so only one of us is on restrictions this Saturday."

"Shh," Jeanmarie ordered. Her heart beat loudly at every creak of the wooden floor. Shadows filled the corners of the hall in spite of the tiny bit of light from the bathroom night-light. She stood in the doorway of the small dorm, barely daring to breathe. Behind her Pearl's breath was warm on her neck. No one stirred. Slowly Jeanmarie made her way past the cots toward the large dresser. She was at the dresser now. Carefully she eased open Sophie's drawer; it squeaked once, making her freeze. She waited, then slipped her hands into the narrow opening and began feeling for the box. After a while she pulled the drawer open wider and searched again. She had felt every inch of the drawer and moved each piece of clothing, feeling for a lump. The box was not there. She'd begun to close the drawer when Pearl tugged hard at the back of her nightgown. Jeanmarie turned to look. Pearl gripped her arm as the two of them stared.

Like someone just getting up for the day, Sophie rose from her bed and headed for the hall. Jeanmarie followed with Pearl right behind her. Sophie must not have seen them. But was she awake or asleep? She was headed down the hall toward the stairs.

"Mrs. Ripple keeps a large chair there as a safety stop just in case," Jeanmarie whispered. "Let's see where she goes," she added. Before either Jeanmarie or Pearl could do anything, Sophie pushed the chair to one side and turned to the stairs. Jeanmarie cried out, "No, no; Sophie, don't!"

Whether Sophie heard her or not Jeanmarie never knew. One second she was at the top of the stairs and the next hurtling down. Pearl screamed, and in another moment, frightened girls were streaming into the hallway. Mrs. Ripple, her long hair tumbling about and a robe flung over her nightgown, flipped on the light switch and hurried down the stairs. All three high-school girls had come running down the attic stairs too, but Jeanmarie and Pearl were already at the lower landing where Mrs. Ripple was kneeling by Sophie.

"You older girls keep the little ones back," Mrs. Ripple called. "See that everyone stays upstairs," she ordered. Sophie lay in a heap. As the housemother bent over her Sophie opened her eyes. "Thank God, she's alive," Mrs. Ripple cried. "Don't try to move, dear. Can you tell me where it hurts?"

"I don't know. Why am I here?" Sophie asked. She looked around, dazed.

Mrs. Ripple held Sophie's hand. "You must have been walking in your sleep and fallen down the stairs. Don't think about it now. Are you in pain?"

To Jeanmarie's shock Sophie pushed herself into a sitting position. "I don't think anything's broken," she said, gingerly feeling her legs. "Ouch; I think I banged my sore foot some. But I don't remember falling." She sounded puzzled.

"Are you sure nothing else hurts?" Mrs. Ripple insisted, examining Sophie's foot. "My dear, it's a miracle that you haven't broken something or worse! I can only guess that because you were sleepwalking you must have fallen without panic and somehow landed without grave damage." She shook her head. "Tomorrow we'll have the nurse check you over to be sure."

"Now that I'm beginning to think about it, I feel like I've been doing belly flops in a swimming pool all day," Sophie said. She stood shakily on her feet supported by Mrs. Ripple's arms. "Maybe I ought to go back to bed," she said weakly.

"Can you manage the stairs if we help?" Mrs. Ripple asked. "Jeanmarie, will you take her other arm, and Pearl, you support her from the back just in case, please." She called up to the crowd of faces above them on the stairs. "It looks like Sophie is going to be all right, girls. Please go back to bed now, all of you. We must be up bright and early in the morning. I don't want to see a single one of you up by the time we reach the top of the stairs."

Slowly, they walked Sophie up one step at a time. When they reached the small dorm and Sophie's cot, the little girls and Leah were already in bed, all of them sitting up. Jeanmarie held Sophie's arm as she lay back against the pillow.

"Oh," Sophie said, reaching under the edge of her pillow. In her hand was the small taped box. "Thanks," she said. "I think I'll be fine now."

"Thank God for his mercy," Mrs. Ripple said, tucking the blanket around Sophie. "Just call me if you need anything."

As Jeanmarie and Pearl followed the housemother into the hall, Jeanmarie sighed. The box was in Sophie's bed all the while.

"I don't know what sort of arrangement we'll need at the head of the stairs, but something more than a chair," Mrs. Ripple said softly. "Run along, girls. I'll see to it that no one falls downstairs again tonight." Mrs. Ripple headed for the armchair Sophie had moved aside, replaced it, and sat down.

Inside their own dorm Pearl whispered, "I've never seen anybody sleepwalking before. It's eerie. I'm glad she didn't break her neck. Is there a cure for sleepwalking?"

"I don't know," Jeanmarie said. "But did you see the box in Sophie's hand just now? She was keeping it under her pillow. I don't know much about sleepwalking, but I do know something important is in that box Sophie's guarding. It has to be the ring."

SIXTEEN

David's Star

Mrs. Ripple stood in the kitchen stirring the breakfast oatmeal when Jeanmarie hurried in to pick up her lunch bag. With a weary smile Mrs. Ripple handed the bag to her with one hand while she continued stirring with the other. "Best move along or you'll be late," she said.

"Thanks," Jeanmarie called, already halfway to the door. The smell of maple syrup wafted from the giant pot of cereal, and Jeanmarie sniffed hungrily. At least it didn't smell burnt this morning. With her lunch bag in her pocket she left, hoping for once she'd reach the farmhouse on time and not have to end up eating half her cheese sandwich before school.

She would have made it if she hadn't forgotten a notebook and run back for it. Mrs. Koppel had glared at the clock as

Jeanmarie entered the farmhouse kitchen. An hour later, with the taste of cheese on her tongue Jeanmarie slipped into class as Mrs. Gillpin began calling the role. Ahead of her Pearl grinned and slid a note onto her desk.

"The school nurse came to see Sophie before school. She's calling her a 'miracle' but says she needs to stay in bed and rest her foot a couple of days. Mrs. Ripple called Dr. Werner, and then Miss Bigler. She asked for Winnie to replace Sophie for the next few days. This is your friendly reporter signing off. S."

Across the way Wilfred looked up as Mrs. Gillpin called Sophie's name. Jeanmarie pretended to read the note in front of her. Should she tell Wilfred about Sophie's accident? From the corner of her eye she watched him pick up his book, push his glasses back on his nose, and begin to read. Good. If Wilfred didn't ask, she wouldn't tell him.

While Mrs. Gillpin read about the wartime food shortage all over Europe Jeanmarie began scribbling in her notebook. Under the words "The Box" she wrote "ring" and then "Sophie." With Sophie guarding the box how could any of them get to it? She penciled a thick line under "Mr. R." How could they help Mrs. Ripple before she left? How soon would she go? A strange thought came to her as she scribbled. What if Mrs. Ripple wasn't going to her family or to a friend's? Mr. R. was her husband. She could be going off with him!

The terrible thought wouldn't leave Jeanmarie. But why would Mrs. Ripple go back to her husband now when she seemed so upset over anything to do with him? She'd kept him a secret all this time at Wheelock. A series of question marks trailed across the page in front of Jeanmarie. She scarcely heard her name called.

"Jeanmarie," Mrs. Gillpin repeated. "Pay attention, please. You are to report to Miss Bigler's office, my dear, right away."

Jeanmarie gulped. Now what had she done? At least it was Miss Bigler's and not Dr. Werner's office, though neither one meant anything good. By the time she reached the office door her heart beat so loudly she could hear it.

In answer to her knock Miss Bigler's voice rang out, "Come in." Jeanmarie walked into the office unsure whether to shut the door behind her or not. "Leave the door open, Jeanmarie. This will only take a moment," Miss Bigler said. "I received a call from Mrs. Koppel. A family matter has come up that requires her presence, and unfortunately there's no one to replace her on such short notice. The farmhouse will not be open for dinner tonight so you will not be needed. You may go directly to Wheelock after school. I should think Mrs. Ripple can put you to work." Miss Bigler's black eyes gave no hint of a smile. "That is all. You may return to class."

Stumbling in her relief Jeanmarie backed her way out of the office and closed the door. She didn't mind helping Winnie at the cottage at all. It would give them both time to think. If they had any time left. Mrs. Ripple might take leave as suddenly as Mrs. Koppel had.

At 3:15 Jeanmarie hurried back to Wheelock, wondering if Mrs. Ripple would still be there. She was. And to Jeanmarie's astonishment, sitting next to her at the kitchen table was Mrs. Shapiro. "It's a sad world," Jeanmarie heard Mrs. Shapiro say as she dabbed at her eyes with a white lace hanky. In front of them was a large plate of Mrs. Shapiro's special prune-filled cookies.

"I really must be going." Mrs. Shapiro stood and smiled at Jeanmarie. "Such a fine house you have here, and a wonderful housemother. So then I'll be seeing you Saturday?" Jeanmarie nodded.

"You must come again," Mrs. Ripple said to Mrs. Shapiro. "And thank you. The girls will love these cookies." The two walked to the door, their heads bent together, their voices low.

Not wanting to be caught eavesdropping, Jeanmarie left the kitchen. She needed to find Winnie anyway. Calling her name she ran lightly up the stairs. In the doorway of the large dorm a tearful Winnie beckoned to her. "Winnie, what is it?" Jeanmarie said, half afraid to know.

"She's really leaving," Winnie said, nearly choking on the words. "When I went to tell her Sophie had a visitor, I saw the suitcase. It's so awful," Winnie groaned.

Jeanmarie's head spun. "But she can't leave now."

"The suitcase isn't packed yet, just lying on the floor waiting," Winnie said. "It means she's getting ready. She hasn't said anything."

If Mrs. Ripple left, Dr. Werner would be forced to call in a substitute. On short notice it might be anyone, including the woman they all called "Matron," who acted more like a jailer than a housemother. "Mrs. Ripple's the best housemother we've ever had, and we've got to help her. There's no time to waste. We have to find that ring," Jeanmarie said.

"Supper is in the oven—baked goulash with eggplant, baked apples for dessert, and brown bread," Winnie said. "We're free until it's time to help serve. I could help you search for the ring, but where? We've already looked every place we could think of."

"Except one," Jeanmarie said. "The box—and Sophie's right on top of it."

"Girls," Mrs. Ripple called from the hallway. "Winnie, I do need you to help me after all. Jeanmarie, since you're home early, why don't you entertain Sophie for a bit?" A surge of anger flashed through Jeanmarie. Entertaining wasn't at all what she had in mind. Clenching her teeth she strode to the small dorm.

Sophie was sitting up in bed and looked up as Jeanmarie entered. "I heard Mrs. Ripple tell you to entertain me," she said. "You needn't bother. Mrs. Shapiro was here earlier to visit." She lowered her eyes and examined something in her hands.

A stack of cards next to Sophie caught Jeanmarie's eye. "I've been wanting to talk to you anyway," Jeanmarie said. "We might as well talk now. I can talk while we play fish. You deal."

Sophie looked up in surprise. She reached for the cards, letting a small silver object drop to her lap as she did. "What could you possibly have to talk to me about?" she asked.

Jeanmarie didn't answer. She stared at Sophie's lap. "David's star! You took David's star. That's why Mrs. Shapiro was crying when I came in. She knows, and she didn't have the heart to accuse you." Jeanmarie stood above Sophie now, so angry she couldn't stop the words. "I saw you that day at the Shapiros', holding the menorah. You would have taken it too if you could have gotten away with it. Why don't you tell the truth for once?"

Sophie stared at her in horror. The cards lay scattered on the floor where they'd fallen. In her hands Sophie clutched the six-pointed star. "It's not David's star," she cried. "It's mine; my Star of David." Like a volcano waiting to explode she erupted. "Star of David, a Jewish star from my mother. If you don't believe me look at the back." Angrily she thrust the star close to Jeanmarie who stared at the words etched on the back. "To Sophie, love, Mama."

"Then you didn't steal it? Mrs. Shapiro didn't come to get it back?" Jeanmarie's voice was low. How could she have been so mistaken?

"I'm Jewish, Jewish!" Sophie cried, pulling the star back to her chest and hugging it tightly. "I only wanted to look at the menorah, hold it." Her voice grew higher. "Do you hear me? I'm Jewish. Mama and Papa were Jewish. I don't care anymore. You all hate me anyway. What difference does it make." Hugging her star in her arms she almost seemed to sway, reminding Jeanmarie of little David grieving over the dead sparrows.

Stunned Jeanmarie knelt next to the bed. "You never meant to steal the menorah, Sophie? You were just looking at it? I'm so sorry. I didn't know." Jeanmarie felt stricken with guilt. "Why didn't you say something?" she pleaded.

Sophie looked at her with eyes full of tears. "How could I?" she wailed. "After my story about my minister papa and the war and everything, I didn't want you to know." Tears streamed in earnest now down her face. "Without Mama and Papa, nobody else had to find out. I don't want to think about Jews being starved to death and Nazis and all. I just want to forget it."

"Oh, Sophie." Jeanmarie cried too now, the tears pouring down as she reached to hold a sobbing Sophie. "I don't hate you; I can't." When the two girls had quieted some and she could speak again, Jeanmarie said, "Mrs. Shapiro said this world is so sad, and she's right, but it's really okay to be Jewish in America. Remember, Jesus was Jewish."

"Yes, he was indeed," said a hearty voice. Both girls turned to look. An elderly gentleman with a round smiling face came into the room. The chaplain. "May I come in?" he asked. In a moment he sat on the edge of Sophie's cot. "I heard about your tumble last night and thought a little visit might be well. It looks like I came just in time." Jeanmarie wiped the tears from her face and stood.

"No, no; sit down, my dear," the chaplain said, and he beamed as Jeanmarie sat again. He gently took the Star of David from Sophie's hand. "How lovely, my dear. So you are Jewish. What a grand privilege to be born Jewish." He smiled broadly as Sophie stared at him. "Oh my, yes. One day, little one, you may learn how much Jesus loved your people." He handed the star back to Sophie. "My dears, there will always be people in this world who do evil and practice hatred, but there are far more who stand up tall for the right. My own son, bless him, is in the army, proud to be fighting against the evils of Hitler's Nazis, and many others with him. One day soon this terrible war will be over." He patted Sophie's head. "We must all be courageous and pray for it to end soon. Meanwhile you need to get better, child. May the shalom of God be with you." He looked at Jeanmarie with a twinkle in his eye. "It's the Jewish word for peace," he explained.

The chaplain told them how he'd visited a Jewish synagogue in New York City when he was a student learning Hebrew.

Sophie's eyes shone. "You know Hebrew?" she asked.

"Yes indeed," he said.

"Papa always prayed in Hebrew," Sophie said.

"Tell me about your folks, child," the chaplain asked gently.

For the next few minutes Jeanmarie listened as Sophie and the chaplain talked.

Finally, the chaplain stood up to go. "I would like to visit again, my dear. Next time, Sophie, maybe we can read from some of David's wonderful Psalms in the Old Testament." He left, promising to return soon. Jeanmarie sat quietly on the edge of Sophie's cot.

Sophie said softly, "My papa would have liked him."

Jeanmarie smiled. "Can I get you something? A drink of water?" Her own throat was dry.

"Well, how about a ribbon so I can wear my Star of David? The clasp on the chain broke, and I'm tired of keeping it hidden in this old box." From under her pillow Sophie held up what had been the taped box. The tape hung loose, the top open. It was empty.

Jeanmarie felt her stomach sink. "You kept the star in that box all this time?"

"Taped up and hidden in my drawer, until last night when I wanted to hold it. I know it won't bring Mama or Papa back, but it's like touching a little part of them." Again tears threatened her eyes. She swallowed hard. "And there's one thing more you ought to know," she said.

Jeanmarie forced herself to look at Sophie. There hadn't been any ring in the box. "Yes," she said, "what is it?"

"I know about the thefts that have been going on around here. I didn't want to say anything before, but I think it's time," Sophie said.

SEVENTEEN

A House for a Mouse

Sophie went on as Jeanmarie waited, hardly daring to breathe. "The day I found Maria's charm bracelet, it was in Lizzie's drawer."

"Lizzie?" Jeanmarie exclaimed. "What on earth?"

"I couldn't believe it either at first. I thought she and May were playing some kind of game. Whatever it was they didn't want anyone else around. A couple of times I saw Lizzie pick up things, silly things like a length of ribbon somebody left in the large washroom and a piece of pink soap. I wondered why she was in the big girls' bathroom at all, but she scooted away before I could ask." Sophie coughed lightly and went on. "Then one day I was coming into the dorm, and I saw her put something shiny that looked like the bracelet Maria lost into

143

her dresser drawer. As soon as I had the chance I looked in Lizzie's drawer, and there it was. When I heard someone coming I stuck the bracelet in my pocket. Later after the spilled juice I went to change my skirt, and it fell out right in front of Maria."

Jeanmarie finished for her, "And she accused you of stealing it. Why didn't you say something?"

Sophie shrugged. "I hadn't talked to Lizzie yet, and anyway, Maria wasn't in the mood to listen."

"None of us listened," Jeanmarie said. She shook her head. "Lizzie is so little, and she's never stolen anything before. I don't understand. Are you sure?" Now she was questioning. "Sorry. You were trying to find out like the rest of us."

"There's only one way to know," Sophie said. "You'll have to ask her."

Jeanmarie stood up. "I need to find her, and fast. There's lots I have to tell you, and I promise I'll be back and fill you in on all of it." Jeanmarie headed to the parlor where the little girls sometimes played games before supper. Did Lizzie have the wedding ring? Where was she? From the kitchen doorway Mrs. Ripple, her white apron rumpled and her face flushed, called to Jeanmarie. "I can use your help too, if you are through visiting with Sophie." Jeanmarie glanced longingly at the parlor door before she answered. "Coming!" she said. Lizzie would have to wait.

On the long table pans of eggplant casserole gave off a strange odor. This was her least favorite food. Mrs. Ripple handed Jeanmarie a large knife. "If you start cutting this pan into squares we can see what is usable and what isn't. I'm afraid I misjudged the oven a bit. Coal stoves are just so difficult at times," she remarked. Mrs. Ripple's red face didn't match her cheerful voice, and Jeanmarie knew she was trying to make light of the over-browned casserole.

They'd saved what they could. Jeanmarie stood next to Winnie as they scrubbed with hard brushes to loosen burnt-on particles from the empty pans. Mrs. Ripple had run upstairs to freshen up before ringing the supper bell. "Winnie, you won't believe what I have to tell you." Winnie stopped work altogether, her eyes wide, while Jeanmarie told her about Sophie. "So all this time we think it's been Lizzie and May who are our thieves."

"Oh no," Winnie said. "Poor, poor Sophie, but Lizzie and May? What will you do? They're the last ones I'd ever have thought would take something. Are you sure?"

It was the very question Jeanmarie had asked Sophie. "I think it's time I had a talk with them to find out," she said. "I can't imagine Lizzie or May stealing, and why would they take things like stamps and bobby pins? Lizzie's wild hair's never seen a bobby pin or May's either." Jeanmarie's hand hovered over the pan she'd been about to scrub. "Lizzie has red hair," she said softly.

"Red hair like the one in your drawer," Winnie added. "Sophie and Lizzie both have red hair! I never thought of it before."

"Me either," Jeanmarie said, finishing her pan. The supper bell rang, and she rinsed her hands. "I'll help you serve, Win," she said.

"When will you talk to them?" Winnie asked as they piled trays with squares of the eggplant casserole.

"After supper, someplace where I can get them alone," Jeanmarie decided.

Under the watchful eye of Mrs. Ripple, who seemed to check every now and then, Jeanmarie, the twins, and Winnie nibbled at their eggplant. Only Pearl absolutely refused and ate her bread instead. As the noise around them grew, Jeanmarie quietly filled in the others on the afternoon's visit with

Sophie. With their heads bent over their food, they listened as Winnie had done with eyes wide. When she'd finished, all of them were staring at the little girls' table across the room where Lizzie sat next to May laughing and talking. Jeanmarie didn't turn to look. Maybe the two little girls really were innocent. She didn't want to listen to her head reminding her of what Sophie had seen. She had to find the truth for herself.

"Don't forget the sparrow," Winnie whispered. "I've saved a bit of green pepper for him, and these crumbs. He's eating almost like one of us." She laughed. Winnie had been on bird duty for the last two days. "He even likes burnt toast."

Jeanmarie smiled as she took the folded napkin with Winnie's offering. "Thanks. I'll feed him first, then find the girls." Instead, the girls found Jeanmarie. Just as she'd replaced the box nest on the window ledge and covered it with its cloth she heard their voices coming down the cellar stairs.

"Lizzie, May, what are you two up to?" Jeanmarie hadn't meant to say that, but she hadn't expected them either. She smiled brightly.

"Oh," Lizzie said. "Nothing. Just playing." She looked at May and nudged her.

"We were just playing," May echoed, nodding her head in agreement.

"What were you playing?" Jeanmarie asked. The two were obviously hiding something.

"That's easy," May blurted. "We're playing mouse house." Lizzie glared at her.

Jeanmarie shook her head. "I don't think I've heard of that one. Tell me, is that why you are down in the cellar? Is your mouse house down here?"

Lizzie looked at her, a solemn expression on her face. "Yup," she said. "But we're not supposed to tell. It's a secret. You won't tell anyone, Nanny, will you?" she begged anxiously.

"If you do, Mrs. Ripple might find out and set a trap and that would be bad," May added.

Jeanmarie took the little girls each by the hand. "Why don't you come and tell me all about it?" she urged. "Do you mean there's a real mouse house down here?" She led the two into the coatroom and sat them down next to her on the floor.

"Well, we're not supposed to say anything," Lizzie said, looking at May, then back to Jeanmarie. "But you're our Nanny, and we know you like mice. You said so, remember?" Puzzled, Jeanmarie tried to think of a time she'd said she liked mice, but she couldn't.

Lizzie reminded her. "Nanny, when you read the story all about the country mouse and the city mouse and showed us the pictures, you said 'what a dear little mouse house.'"

Jeanmarie did remember the story. She'd read it to them so long ago she'd forgotten what the pictures looked like. "But what has all that got to do with your mouse house?" When the girls kept silent, Jeanmarie pleaded. "I really would like to know," she urged.

"Tell her," May said.

"But you have to promise not to do anything to scare them," Lizzie demanded.

"I promise," Jeanmarie said, trying to keep the eagerness from her voice.

"Okay, then follow me." The two girls stood and Lizzie led the way into the storage room, past the cupboards that held the winter's jars of fruit and vegetables put up last summer, and around the corner behind the floor-to-the-ceiling cupboard. May fished a flashlight from her pocket, turned it on, and laid it carefully down near the corner wall. "See there," Lizzie whispered.

In the corner where the wall met the floor was a small mouse hole. Over the years at the orphanage Jeanmarie had seen enough of them to recognize it right away. This one, unlike the others mended by one of the older boys who served as the orphanage's carpenter, was new to her. "So that's your mouse house," she whispered. She'd bent down to look and stayed on her knees next to the two little girls squatting to peer into the hole. "Now what do we do?" she asked, keeping her voice low. "You haven't told me how to play the game yet."

Lizzie reached into her pocket and pulled out a length of string, an old piece of cork, and several crusts of bread. "This is what we do," she said, pushing the items into the hole. After a few seconds of peering inside she sat back. "There," she said. "The string is just what she needs for a new clothesline, and the cork will make a good footstool. It's hard, you know, to dry things in winter," she added.

Jeanmarie swallowed hard. "What else have you put down there, Lizzie?" she asked.

"Oh, lots of things," May offered. "Pretty pictures for her wall, a warm rug, and clothespins, all kinds of things."

In spite of her fears Jeanmarie couldn't picture what May was saying. "But how on earth did you fit clothespins into that hole? And pictures?"

"Oh, Nanny," Lizzie said, "not real clothespins, bobby pins." Lizzie stopped abruptly and searched Jeanmarie's face.

"Lizzie, where did you find the bobby pins?" Jeanmarie demanded. Lizzie didn't answer. "Look at me, Lizzie, please." Jeanmarie lifted the little girl's chin. Lizzie said nothing. "I think I know where the bobby pins came from, so maybe you better tell me," Jeanmarie ordered.

"We were going to put them back, truly," Lizzie said. Her mouth quivered. "It rained so hard, and we had to find something Miss Mouse could use to dry out things. May found a spool of thread, and I remembered the bobby pins. We couldn't let anyone know the secret, so I just borrowed them." Lizzie hung her head.

Gently, Jeanmarie lifted the little girl's chin again. "How were you planning to put them back?"

"That's the trouble," Lizzie said in a low voice. "I forgot, and then when we put the stick down and all the other things, we couldn't see them anymore."

Jeanmarie let go of Lizzie's chin. "Didn't you think of me, that I needed those pins? I really do, and now I'll have to wait until sometime when I can buy more, if I can."

May looked ready to cry but still said nothing.

Two big tears slid down Lizzie's face. "We didn't mean to do wrong," she said.

"And the pictures?" Jeanmarie prodded. She'd already guessed.

"Stamps," May whispered. "I said we could loan them to her for the winter, and then when spring came she wouldn't need them anymore. Mice like to camp out in the spring and summer," she said. With a sad tone she added, "Only like Lizzie said, we couldn't get anything back out, and we're too big to see way into the hole, so we don't know where her living room is either."

Jeanmarie nearly smiled but said, "First of all you both are old enough to know that you don't go looking in someone else's dresser drawers or things without asking permission. Never mind about keeping the mouse house secret. You ought to have asked for things and just said you needed them for something. You know the orphanage doesn't give us stamps and pins and thread and ribbons. We have to work for them. I'm guessing you two took all those things?" Looking miserable, the two girls nodded.

"If someone took something that belonged to one of you without asking, what would you call that?" Jeanmarie demanded.

"Stealing?" whispered Lizzie.

"Yes," Jeanmarie replied, "and you two nearly got Sophie into terrible trouble." As plainly as she could she explained.

Both little girls were crying in earnest now. Jeanmarie let them cry until gradually with a final hiccup they'd quieted. "You must never ever steal anything again," she said sternly. "I know you're sorry. Now it's very important that you tell me everything. Just what did you take and where is it all?"

Aided by May, Lizzie listed all the small items they'd taken or found. Jeanmarie listened carefully. When they finished she said, "But you didn't mention Mrs. Ripple's scissors or her small black leather change purse."

"Didn't see them," Lizzie said. "Mrs. Ripple asked all of us, but honest, May and me didn't take them. They couldn't have fit down the hole, and anyway, we wouldn't take Mrs. Ripple's good things."

Jeanmarie groaned. It meant the purse and the ring were still missing! "I guess you didn't see a ring either?" she asked hopefully.

Lizzie and May looked at each other, each shaking her head. "No ring," Lizzie said.

"Wait a minute," Jeanmarie ordered. "What do you know about Maria's charm bracelet, the one with the little fish on it?"

Lizzie's eyes grew wider. "The bracelet?"

May gulped. "Lizzie found it, but it disappeared," she said.

"I found it behind the chair in the parlor, and we were going to give it right back, but May said we ought to at least show it to Miss Mouse. I thought we could hang it from the stick, just long enough so she could have a nice look at it. But when I went to get it from my drawer it was gone. Truly," she added.

Jeanmarie covered her face with her hands. She couldn't believe all these weeks two small thieves had been decorating a mouse hole with their things. A small hand tugged at hers. "Nanny, we promise we'll never do it again, never."

Jeanmarie looked at them. "I promised you I wouldn't frighten the mice, and I didn't. But you both know you did something wrong, and even though you're sorry, and I'm sure you won't do it again, you're going to have to tell Mrs. Ripple." At the look on Lizzie's face Jeanmarie said quickly, "Of course now that it's spring, you know Miss Mouse has already found herself a nice campsite somewhere in the woods. I'm certain you don't have a thing to worry about." Her words seemed to work magic in the children's expressions. Curious, she asked, "By the way, how did you find this mouse hole?"

Lizzie explained on the way up the stairs. "First May saw Miss Mouse running across the coatroom floor right into the storage room. When we looked we found the hole."

Mrs. Ripple was in her sewing room. Jeanmarie pushed the two little girls toward the door, whispered, "Be brave now," and left. Except for poor Sophie and the missing wedding ring the whole thing might have been plain funny. She had to tell the others and Sophie. Behind her she heard the door close. If only Mrs. Ripple's problem could be solved as easily as Lizzie and May's mouse house.

EIGHTEEN

A Night of Confession

Jeanmarie faced the little group gathered around Sophie's bed. She'd explained everything, and then Sophie had told her story. A deep sadness filled Jeanmarie as Sophie told the others about her real folks. Winnie sat closest to Sophie. Her round face streaked with tears, she'd reached out to hold Sophie's hand. Pearl wiped the wetness from her own eyes. Tess and Maria held each other's hand tightly.

"Papa loved to go to the tailor shop and work the old sewing machine," Sophie said. "Sometimes he brought bits of material home, and Mama would laugh and put them together for a quilt. If only they hadn't gone to work together that morning. I never saw them again after the car ran them down." She added softly, "I miss them so much."

Winnie patted her hand. "I don't know who my folks were, but I wish I could have known your mama and papa."

Pearl cleared her throat. "We're all the family we've got now. We need to stick together, right?" She looked directly at Sophie.

"Right," the twins echoed.

"All for one, one for all," Jeanmarie added. "You're one of us now, Sophie."

Sophie dried her eyes with the hanky Winnie handed her. "Thanks, all of you," she said. "I guess with everything out in the open we can all start over—including Lizzie and May." She smiled.

Jeanmarie smiled too at the thought of the mouse hole filled with stuff. By now the two little girls had confessed. Except for one big item—the ring. "We still don't know where Mrs. Ripple's things went, or her ring," she said. "If no one took them, where are they?" She thought of the trash. If they'd accidentally fallen into the trash that was burned weekly, it was too late. Or were they lying out of sight in some corner? "If we don't find them there's no way we can keep her from leaving," she said.

"Even if we do find the ring she might go anyway," Pearl stated. "How else can she get away from her husband?"

Sophie's eyes were big with surprise. "I thought Mrs. Ripple was a widow, like most of the other housemothers."

Jeanmarie explained and added, "So without the wedding ring we don't have anything to make him go away." No one said anything under the gloom that fell like a shadow over them.

"We could beg her to stay," Winnie offered timidly.

"You mean tell her the truth?" Pearl asked.

"Look at us," Sophie said. "Once everything came out in the open it helped."

A plan tugged at Jeanmarie as she thought about telling Mrs. Ripple what they knew. "Suppose we all went to her; we could tell her that we know about Mr. Ripple and that we want her to stay. Then we could tell her our plan." She looked around at the others. "We could find ways to keep her safe right here. She never has to see him again if she doesn't want to. We can still write a letter warning him of serious trouble if he comes here again." She paused. "We can take turns on phone duty so one of us answers the phone before she does. And if it's him we'll get rid of him." Jeanmarie waited for the rest to think about the plan. It was all they could do without the missing ring. One by one the others agreed.

Sophie had insisted on coming with them. They were just in time to see Lizzie and May about to leave Mrs. Ripple's sewing room. "Girls, what is all this?" Mrs. Ripple exclaimed. "Sophie, why aren't you in your bed?"

Jeanmarie took charge. "Please, Mrs. Ripple, we all have something to say."

"Well, I suppose I had better listen. Lizzie and May have finished their visit. You may go, girls." She motioned the small girls out.

Without thinking, Jeanmarie cried, "Wait. I mean, please, can they stay? In a way they're part of this too."

Mrs. Ripple looked grave. "I'm not sure I like the sound of that, but come in, all of you. Sit wherever you can. Now what is this all about?"

Jeamarie swallowed hard. "We know about Mr. Ripple."

Mrs. Ripple gave a start. Her hand went to her throat. "You know?"

"We met him the other day," Jeanmarie said, "and the night he was here I bumped into him. Of course, I didn't have any idea he was your husband then."

"My husband?" Mrs. Ripple said in a choked voice.

Pearl quickly assured her, "It was the hotel stationery, the envelope, that gave us the clue we needed. When Jeanmarie phoned the hotel clerk pretending to check on a bill from the hotel for you, he told us it was Mr. Ripple who owed the hotel a large sum. Once we knew you weren't a widow, and the letters that upset you so much were from him, we put it all together." She finished breathlessly.

"Right," Jeanmarie agreed. "We don't want you to leave, Mrs. Ripple, please." A chorus of pleases echoed her. "And we think we have a plan that will work. We wanted to find your lost change purse and the wedding ring, but we couldn't. We thought Mr. Ripple might be after money to pay his debts, and he could sell the ring if he promised to leave you alone." Mrs. Ripple looked stunned. "Don't worry," Jeanmarie went on. "Once he receives a letter warning him that we're onto him, I don't think he'll be back. We'll answer the phone and make sure he doesn't want to come. You never need to see him again, honest. Please don't leave us." Her voice faded to a stop.

Mrs. Ripple sat back in her chair. After a moment of silence, she stood and went into her bedroom. She returned, carrying a small framed picture in her hands; she set it on her sewing table facing out to the room. Jeanmarie saw a young man in a sailor's uniform. He was broad shouldered, a giant of a man, with a kind smile. Jeanmarie knew right away she would have liked him. "My husband," Mrs. Ripple announced clearly.

"As you can see," she said, "he is nothing at all like the Mr. Ripple who was here." Picking up the picture she held it for a minute, then put it back. "We were married two days before he left for duty. We didn't have much, just a small wedding. After his first tour we planned to hold a big family affair. We couldn't afford a real wedding ring, so I wore his school ring. I keep it here." Reaching inside the neck of her blouse she pulled a long delicate chain from it. Hanging from it was a wide-band silver ring with a square front. "You see, we thought one day I'd have a real wedding ring. But the war came suddenly, and my husband lost his life in the bombing of Pearl Harbor."

Jeanmarie gasped.

"Yes," Mrs. Ripple continued. "I am a widow, girls. Now let me confess something to you. You are right that the young man you met is Mr. Ripple. He is my husband's younger brother, Jim." This time Jeanmarie groaned. "It's true that I certainly have been upset by his letters and phone calls, to say nothing of his two visits here. However you discovered his faults with money, you are correct. Jim wasn't always that way. We were all a close family, and after their father's death, my husband was like a father to Jim and their sister, Hattie. I would give anything to help him, but I'm afraid the character defects he has will take a stronger hand than mine."

"But you're leaving," Jeanmarie said.

"Yes and no," Mrs. Ripple stated. "It's about time our family had a meeting with this young man to straighten out some things. I do plan to go to Hattie's for a week. We've asked Jim to come, and if he really wants help, he shall have to come and listen to our conditions." Warmth flooded Jeanmarie's face. Mrs. Ripple leaned over and touched Jeanmarie's shoulder. "Not everything is the way it looks on the surface, my dear," she said. "I should have let you all know the purse and scissors turned up in a drawer I'd forgotten about."

"But I was so sure." Jeanmarie shook her head. "We really messed up this time," she said. She didn't add that it was mostly her fault. In the corner of the room someone giggled, and Jeanmarie turned to see Sophie clap her hands over her mouth. In a second others were laughing. Even Mrs. Ripple. Jeanmarie laughed until her sides ached. "No missing wedding ring," she said, barely able to speak, "and no terrible husband."

Mrs. Ripple dried her eyes as the laughter finally settled down. "What do you say we all go downstairs for some war cake I was saving as a surprise?"

In the kitchen between bites of the savory cake, Jeanmarie made a decision. "I think I better make a last confession," she said. Stillness rippled across the room. "There's a bird in the cellar. He's only a baby sparrow, and I've been taking good care of him," she went on. "He'll be able to fly soon." She looked at Mrs. Ripple's face, searching for a sign.

Carefully, Mrs. Ripple put down her piece of cake. "You are talking about the bird with the splinted wing? The one who's nesting on our window ledge?" Jeanmarie stared at her. "Yes, Jeanmarie, I found him quite by accident. I'd hoped someone would soon claim the poor little fellow."

"You're not angry then?" Jeanmarie felt relief wash over her.

"This has been a night of confession, and we shall let it go this time," Mrs. Ripple said. The half-smile around her mouth said more.

Back upstairs in the dorm Jeanmarie lay on her cot in the semidarkness. None of them were asleep yet. "At least nobody is on restrictions this weekend," she said. "We should make some plans."

"Oh no," Pearl called from across the room. "No plans."

"Well, it's just that I've been thinking how we could find out if Ralph made it to his uncle's," Jeanmarie urged.

"No plans. Go to sleep, Jeanmarie," the twins said in unison. Jeanmarie smiled. She could wait.

More about This Book

Jeanmarie and the Missing Ring is set in the final year of the war with Germany and the Axis powers. Fighting continued on many battlefronts overseas. On the home front the United States called for more men for the armed forces, tightened rationing on items such as meat and coal, and urged Americans to save all scrap paper, metal, and fats for the war effort. Newsreels brought pictures of the war home, and it was these especially that made clear the terrible plight of the Jewish people.

Hitler's plan to exterminate all Jews in countries conquered by Germany brought great suffering and death to the Jews of Europe. Even when Germany was about to lose the war, Hitler continued the killing of Jewish people. A total of six million Jews were put to death simply because they were

Jewish. Though Sophie and David are fictional characters, like them, Jewish people in the United States felt the fear and sorrows of the terrible fate of so many Jewish men, women, and children. Today in America, respecting others of different faiths and races is an important part of being an American. For readers who would like to know more about the plight of the Jews during the war, *The Diary of Anne Frank* is the true story of a Jewish girl who hid from the Nazis.

In the story of *Jeanmarie and the Missing Ring*, the menorah mentioned in chapter ten is similar to the one used in Jewish homes each year during the celebration of Hanukkah. The holiday comes close to the Christmas holidays. Jewish children receive gifts, play games, and remember the story of Hanukkah, a time in Jewish history when the Jewish people were rescued from their enemies. The feast lasts eight days, and candles are lit each night. The ninth candle of the menorah is called the Shamash and is used to light the other candles.

The Star of David that belongs to Sophie and David in our story is a six-pointed star used on the flag of Israel. It is a Jewish symbol that was used in the Middle Ages by some Jews but became popular in the ninth century as an emblem of Judaism. In Hebrew it is called Magen David or Shield of David, meaning God was the protector of ancient Israel's King David.

The prayer called the Kaddish, mentioned in chapter fourteen, is a prayer said for someone who has died. It is a prayer the mourner says in praise of God and is also called the mourner's prayer.